Dreamers in
CHESHIRE BAY

USA TODAY BESTSELLING AUTHOR
H.M. SHANDER

To Kelly G, Rachel C, and Shawna W.
Thank you for your feedback and thoughts.
Hope you fall in love with M&Z even more now.
HMS

Table of Contents

Chapter One

The bakery tantalized the tastebuds and got the salivary glands working overtime with the rich cinnamon aroma, and the aromatic scent of melted butter. With two freshly made cinnamon buns on my tray, and two mugs of steaming black coffee with just a smidge of cream, I set the tray on the dainty bistro table by the window.

"Compliments of Aunt Sylvia," I said, sliding into the seat across from my best friend, Ashley.

She cupped her hands around her mouth. "Thanks, Aunty Sylvia."

The bakery was deserted, for now, as it had only opened five minutes prior. The upcoming lunch rush would surely pack the place.

Aunt Sylvia, who was everyone's adopted aunt, poked her handkerchief-covered head out from behind the glass display, and practically clucked at Ashley. "You're most welcome, darling. You need to come visit more often."

"Yes, ma'am. Been busy working."

"Never too busy to come and grab a takeout." Aunt Sylvia

put her hands on her ample hips. In a minute, there was going to be a finger waving about.

"No, ma'am. Next week, I promise."

"Always room for you, darling."

"Thank you." Ashley faced me and took a sip of her coffee, and then it on the saucer.

Sylvia's Bakery was quaint in that respect, mugs with saucers, tiny butter knives to go with any personal loaf.

"Yeah, but she loves you like the daughter she never had." I raised my own cup and tipped my head in the direction of where she was loading a tray of goodies into the display case.

Sylvia had two grown boys, who took off out of our small town as fast as their legs could carry them. They had huge dreams in the big city, and sadly, for Sylvia's broken heart, they never ventured home very often. Once they were gone, she practically adopted her regulars as family, and in her books, I was practically a full-blooded niece, aside from the differences in our skin tones; her's a gorgeous ebony colouring which contrasted with my pale peach.

Ashley tucked a strand of her beautiful chestnut coloured hair behind her ear, punctuated with seven earrings, including a helix and a tragus, which I was never brave enough to get done. "So, what's on the agenda today?"

I crossed my legs, picking off a few cat hairs from my nylons. "Well, I'm meeting an old-sounding man who's interested in the ole Lowell place." I picked the edge of the cinnamon bun, the thick layer of frosting coating my fingertips. "He's a bit of a grump."

"A grump?"

"Yeah, he sounds real likeable on the phone." I rolled my eyes. "All business, but at least he avoids the small chat. Quickly gets down to the bullet points and is gone. His emails are just as quick. If they contained fifty words, I'd be shocked. Anyway, he just wants to see the property in person before he signs off on it."

"So, he's taking it?"

"I'm assuming today's meeting is just a formality. He's had the inspector through, and nothing was out of place. It is a lot of money, so I'm guessing he just wants to make sure his investment isn't a total waste." Shrugging, and after picking another piece, I licked the gooey cinnamon spread from my fingertip. Damn, Aunt Sylvia had the market on these bad boys.

Fingers clean, I continued. "That's too bad the town couldn't buy it, and it had to go onto the market. Would be great to put a museum or something wonderful on the land."

In my dreams, I could imagine a thousand different scenarios for the place, but instead, the family listed it, and it sold to the highest bidder, not that there had been a lot of interest.

Ashley cut her cinnamon bun with a fork and knife. I shook my head at the lunacy of it.

"You know," she said, "Cheshire Bay is pretty tapped out for money, but there is that bronze bust in the central park from last year."

I shrugged, as if that made it all better.

"We can barely fix sidewalks and roadways." Ashley was part of the three-person part time town council. "Or install a flashing pedestrian crosswalk. And you know where we could get an influx of surplus cash? Outsider brands and franchisers. We need them to buy the vacant lands and turn them into something amazing."

"Hey, I'm on board for a little more money, since I know our tax dollars are stretched pretty thin, but that would ruin our little corner of the world. Adding in the kind of businesses you're talking about; it opens the doors to needing to add stoplights. Corporations will take away from our charm, and we don't need that shit here. They can keep it in Stewart Surf."

"We need a stoplight, or at minimum a flashing pedestrian light. Thankfully, no one's been hit." She lifted the cup to her mouth.

"And let's hope it stays that way. I don't want our town to change. Ever."

Ashley stared out the window of Sylvia's Bakery onto Main Street. "You're getting your wish, for now. Aside from a few business facelifts, this place hasn't changed since the late seventies. We're due. Overdue, in fact."

Which, for the most part, was true. The majority of the shops in town were original, although only a handful still had original owners. Most though had passed the business down to other family members.

"The right influx of business…" She led off and stopped herself from saying more by stuffing in a huge piece of cinnamon bun.

I shook my head. "Please don't tell me town council is tinkering with the idea of letting the franchises in?"

"Well, it's on the table. Maybe even something more." She leaned closer after scanning the area. We were still alone. "This is on the down low, but recently, an investor has teased us with the possibility of setting up a new motel, something that caters more to the tourists, and less to the transient residents."

"No." I shook my head. "I hope you told them to shove it."

While it was true the only motel within walking distance of the beach was in dire need of a makeover, there was no way the town would sell out to the masses. It was part of Cheshire Bay's charm. That, and how town council years ago enacted a no-franchise policy. Unless you were an independent, you couldn't get permits in the town. They'd made sure of it.

"We need to stay wholesome and innocent. Let Stewart Surf have all the trendy, tacky, and tested franchises, and leave us alone." Just the very idea made my blood boil.

"Mia, relax." She put her hand on mine. "I'm just saying. Updating the motel, if that's what the investor plans, would bring more tourists to this part of the peninsula, and that would have a profound impact to the local businesses."

"And also a huge drain on our limited resources." I stared at my best friend, pulling my hand away. "You're on the side of the big bad business, aren't you?"

"I'm just saying it would be good for the town." She shrugged.

"Stewart Surf can, and does, have all of that. It's less than thirty minutes away. We don't need it here."

"Well, a proposal is coming before council on the fifteenth. If you're so passionately against it, you should attend. Make an informed decision, rather than an emotional one."

"I hate politics, you know that."

"Yes, I do, but you should still come and hear what they have to say."

"They? Who are they?"

"The corporate shirts, flying in on their private jet."

"Ugh." I rolled my eyes and tore a piece of cinnamon bun.

That's all the town needed. At least my eleven o'clock buyer wasn't into that. The old man only wanted the five-acre property at the end of Beach Bay road, and you can't do much with that.

Before I'd met Ashley, I'd parked my car in front of A Whole New World, only the greatest bookstore in the whole Bay area, maybe even the whole of Vancouver Island. Perhaps that was because it was owned by my adopted brother, Adam, who took over after Grandpa died a few years back. Since Sylvia's Bakery was only a leisurely stroll away, and after eating the sugar loaded baked goods, the short walk back did me good.

I rounded the corner off Main Street, passed the little kids' boutique – Belles et Garcons, and onto First Avenue, named since it was the first avenue of downtown, even though it was the most central avenue of the area. It also boasted many dangling lights strung across the road, giving it a unique look in the evenings. I'd had high hopes the local businesses on Main Street would adopt the look, but so far, they hadn't.

Click-clacking in my heels past the stores, I waved to the townsfolk milling about.

"Good morning," I'd call out.

"Morning, Miss MacDonald," most would reply, or at the very least wave back.

I loved this town, and the friendliness that greeted me.

As I approached Second Street, I saw a complete stranger standing outside the bookstore, casually glancing at Adam's book display of the month.

Every month A Whole New World had a new window theme. Being that we were approaching spring, he had out a mini-garden display, with a real-life garden and several How-To books perched around it. Wonder what he was growing? A sunflower maybe? Or tulips? It was hard to tell from the little sprig of greenery poking through the soil.

Casually, I walked up the handsome man dressed in jeans

and a white tee, with a navy blazer over top. There was no way this was my eleven o'clock.

"You look lost, can I help you? Cheshire Bay isn't too big; I can help you find what you're looking for."

"No, not lost. I'm waiting on someone." His voice was gravelly, like he hadn't spoken in a while, and he gave me a solid once over.

Compared to him, I was a tad overdressed in my pencil skirt, blouse, and wrap.

"You aren't Ms. MacDonald by chance?"

"You're here to see the Lowell place?" Maybe the old man I'd spoken on the phone with had sent his grandson, because there was no way this was him. This guy was slightly older than my fresh start into my thirties at best. Well groomed, pleasant on the eyes. Certainly not looking as old as he sounded when he talked with me on the phone.

"Yes, I'm Zachary Newton-Garcia."

Well shut the front door. My day just got a whole lot better.

Chapter Two

I extended my hand in greeting. Although I desperately needed a manicure, the lotion I applied daily still kept my skin soft and supple, plus it was strawberry daquiri scented, a favourite.

Zachary Newton-Garcia shook it, but didn't exert his manliness into a death squeeze, something of which I was quite appreciative. His hands were cool and had a softness to them suggesting a desk job of sorts, and there was a definite absence of a wedding ring.

"Pleasure to finally put a face to the name," he said, clearing his throat. "Please forgive me, I'm just getting over a bad cold, and although I am fine otherwise, it's still lingering and affecting my voice."

That explained the old man voice on the other end of the line last week.

"Well, since you're likely to be a new resident here, you could always swing by Dr. Singh's office, he's a family doctor, and see if he can help you." I pointed south. "It's just off Main Street, but you may have to wait until tomorrow as sometimes his walk ins are jam packed. Depends on how long you're willing to wait." One town doctor wasn't enough some days, but he was worth the wait.

"Good to know, but I'm only here for a couple of days to check out the property and town, then I need to head back."

"To Vancouver, correct?"

"Correct." He looked so deep into my eyes I was worried he could truly see my soul.

Needing the distraction, I grabbed the keys from my purse and double-clicked the remote to unlock the doors of my car parked just up the road.

"Shall we?" I pointed to my squeaky-clean car. "Well, personally, I think you'll see Cheshire Bay is a completely different way of life than the big city. Hop in, and I'll give you a quick tour of my town before I show you the property in person."

Zachary climbed into the passenger seat as I slid into the driver's spot and cleared his throat. "Looking forward to it."

After tossing my purse onto the dash, I pointed to the complimentary water bottle in the cup holder. "Please help yourself."

"Thanks. This is perfect." He cracked the top and took a swig. "Haven't had anything to drink since leaving this morning."

"Did you fly in?"

"Yes."

"And I'm not a good flyer. I get a little nauseous, so I try to book flights out in the morning before I've eaten." He tipped back the bottle and chugged at least half of it before securing the lid and setting it back into the cup holder.

"There's a little plastic bag in the glove box if you feel the need to, you know, toss your cookies."

"I'll be fine now that I'm back on the ground."

With a side-eyed glance at my passenger, I put the car into

gear and drove forward on the street, only to back into the alleyway so I could turn around; the road wasn't big enough for a proper U-turn, not with cars lining both sides. "Since you haven't eaten, are you hungry? I can stop somewhere while you run in and grab something."

"Honestly, I'm fine, for now, but thank you."

"Sure thing. You holler if you need anything."

He rolled the window down an inch, allowing his light fragrance – an expensive scent, like Bergamot or some exotic spice – to tease the confines of the interior. I rather enjoyed the way it changed the air in my car – smelling it all would not bother me in the least.

"Eric Morris, was he your pilot?" I stopped at the stop sign, and flipped my head left and right. When it was all clear, I advanced and turned left onto Main Street. With no stop lights in the town, I always made sure it was safe.

"Sounds about right."

"He's one of my friends. Actually, he owns a house down the road from the Lowell's place."

"Nice." He nodded.

"That's the property you've been eyeing. Old Man Lowell, or Frederick Lowell to be proper, was the founding father of Cheshire Bay. He moved here back in the 40s or 50s, and slowly built the town I'm about to show you. He died not too long ago, and his family wasn't interested in keeping the property."

Which I never understood, unless it was for financial reasons, but still. It was an iconic place. Regardless, they listed it, and my passenger, scooped it up offering a deal above list.

"You'll find that everyone knows everyone else via like one or two people." I inched down Main Street, stopping as a group of pedestrians sauntered across the road, bags in hand. "It's like a six degrees of separation thing, but half that, if you're lucky."

My car rolled on past a few shops, the owners propping open their doors for the start of the day. Most stores opened around ten, a leisurely way to start the day. No rush, no fuss. Except Sylvia's bakery, she typically opened at nine.

"The places in Cheshire Bay have unique names, like Whimsical Whims and Daisy's Delights. Peter's Pita is on the street behind, and he makes the best donairs."

"I love a good donair."

"You will not be disappointed, trust me on this." I nodded and watched him from the corner of my eye, giving him a quick full body scan.

Zachary was taking in the front shop windows, his ringless hand on his thigh.

I pointed to the end of downtown, on Sixth Street. "If you follow that road to the left, you'll get to our harbour. A few boats dock there in the summer, and it's nice if you like to boat watch. We get some pretty sizable vessels from time to time. Once we had a grand yacht, but only once. Apparently, that channel is too shallow for the big mother boats."

"Good to know. I'll leave my big boat at home." He chuckled as he faced me.

I liked him already. A tad quiet, but funny.

I continued to point out the way. "That's the road to our only dance bar in town – the Cowboy Den. It's a total dive of a place, but they have cheap drinks and a decent dance floor, if that thing appeals to you. My little sister works there as one of the waitresses." He didn't give off any cowboy vibes, and didn't seem much to care for that, so I kept up with the verbal tour. "Do you have any family?"

"Ah, no. Recently divorced, no kids."

"Oh, I'm sorry."

"I'm not." It rolled out with a snort.

Grimacing, I pointed to the road signs. "Well, Birch Bay Burgers is known as a family restaurant, but it's still a lovely place to go as a single. Or on a date."

The left edge of his lip twitched.

"There's the road leading to our fine dining establishment called the Harbour Chophouse. Best steaks in town. Or on the island at least."

Zachary didn't say much but covered a cough.

I waved as I passed by a middle-aged woman. "There's Dr. Johnson. She's the local veterinary. Do you have any pets?"

After a quick drink, he shook his head. "No time for pets. Too busy. You?"

"Just a Calico. That's a cat."

A smirk pushed up his right cheek. "I know what a Calico is."

I shrugged playfully. "You just seem like you'd be more of a dog lover, especially buying the Lowell place. Lots of room for a big dog."

"Maybe some day, but not in the immediate future. What's your cat's name?" He cleared his throat.

"Callie."

"Callie the Calico. Cute. I like it." A wink, on the tip of a feathered arrow, shot in my direction, and my heart responded with an unfamiliar flutter.

What was going on with me? I shouldn't be interested in this guy.

Firstly, he was a client, not that there was anything in a code of conduct book about relationships with clients, but still. It skewed the professionalness and could be somehow seen as a conflict of interest.

Secondly, he didn't live here – yet. He lived on the mainland, and not that it was even on the table, long-distance relationships weren't my jam.

Thirdly, he was clearly happy about his divorce which likely meant he wasn't interested in dating. Not that he was interested, but that wink did something to me. Sure, I could rationalize it by saying he did it to everyone, and maybe he was a huge womanizer and a reason why he was happy to be divorced, as he wasn't a one-woman kind of guy.

Perhaps though, I was reading way too much into things, because it had been that long since a guy had winked at me, let alone smiled and had what could barely be considered conversation.

Yes, I was lonely for man company, but I needed to get a hold of myself.

I focused back on the road, swallowing a fresh inhale of spicy aftershave.

"Well, that concludes our tour. We're now on the southern end of Cheshire Bay." I drove into a nearby parking lot and put the car into park. "All told, the town is only about six kilometers long, but it's just the right size. It's perfect." I pulled out a printed map from the back seat and handed it to my charming guest, who was taking in every single word I breathed. "This here highlights all the walking trails along the coast, and the two lighthouses, although one is decommissioned. It stopped working back in 1997, and a new one was erected immediately afterwards, but in a different location as it was better. They also added a lovely park beside it, so it's a wonderful place for sunset picnics. Although," I tipped my head as a memory came back. "The view from the decommissioned one is great too."

A smile stretched across his clean-cut face. "I'll keep that in mind."

"It's really something else. Plus, if you get lucky, you may see a whale or two as we have a few pods native to the area. Did you know that?" He shook his head but maintained steady eye contact. "However, if you want a whale watching tour, you'd be best served to head north to Stewart Surf. They're the only ones that have the tours. Oh! Ask for Landon Morris – he's Eric, your pilot's brother. Older? Younger?" I swiped my hand through the air. "It doesn't matter. But Landon is a Cheshire Bay resident, so I'm happy to promote his business, plus, you may run into Harrison."

"Who's that?"

"Oh, he's my brother. Works with Landon. Landon owns and operates; Harrison just works there."

Tapping his temple, he nodded. "All noted. You really love your hometown, don't you?"

I sagged into my seat as a broad smile stretched out my lips and highlighted my straight teeth – a 21st birthday gift to myself. "I really do."

A couple, hand in hand, strolled down the sidewalk toward the ocean. At the end of the sidewalk, there was a small beach with a few logs. Not as nice as some of the others, but it was a nice place to sit and relax.

"Lived here long?" Zachary's question snapped me back to the interior of the car.

"My whole life. My honorary aunt runs Sylvia's Bakery, the best bakery on the island, and really on the whole island, if I'm being truthful."

"Are you?"

"Try something from there and you tell me." I grabbed my silky-smooth hair and pulled it over my left shoulder.

The air crackled with electricity, and if I didn't know better, I'd say he was fighting against another smile. They came easy to him.

"I'm guessing with this much zest for small town living, you must be the oldest in your family?" The question came with a raised brow.

"Actually, I'm an only child."

His brows furrowed. "But you've mentioned siblings."

"I'm adopted. Kind of a weird story, and I'll tell you another time, as it's a long conversation."

"How many are there of you?"

"Oh there's just me."

He laughed. "I meant in your adopted family."

"Including me, there's five."

"Five?" He covered his mouth and coughed. "Sorry. Wow. There's just my parents and me. They didn't have time for anyone else." Was there a hint of sadness with his words?

"Aw, that's too bad. Siblings are great. Sure, we tussled and had our moments of angst, but overall, it's so nice to have a lifelong buddy. Or four buddies, as I have it." I put the car in gear and pulled back out onto the main road.

Cheshire Bay had one singular main road, and all the other roads branching off eventually rejoined again, so it was impossible to get lost. Even my best friend, who was directionally challenged, could find her way. You just kept driving until you arrived back on Main Street again. A sweet perk of the small town.

"Alright, are you ready to see your possible new home?"

"Oh yes. Not sure how it tops all this." He waved toward the windshield, the tiny town stretched out before us.

19

"If I'm rambling, please let me know." It was a quirk of mine, and the deep Italian in me often reared as I talked with my hands. Ashley joked if I had to sit on my hands, I'd be the quietest one around. I needed them to talk and express myself.

"You are, but I love it."

I studied his expression quickly. There was nothing but truth settling over it. "How's that?"

"I've never met anyone who loves her town as much as you do." He twisted in his seat and leaned against the door.

"This place is perfect; idyllic and tranquil. I love it here. The stone and brick buildings are original, at least most of them, but it adds to the nostalgia. Sure, our roadways need a little work, but that's a maintenance problem, and every place has that, show me a town or city that doesn't?" I held my breath, waiting for a response that never came. "We have the best beaches within an easy drive, a suspension bridge over a gorgeous ravine, and some taller hills for a little variety. We have everything here, and…" I slapped his thigh without thinking. "We have the best weather."

His eyes widened and I realised what I did.

"Ohmygod, I'm so sorry." I covered my mouth, my own eyes threatening to bug out of my head. "I just got too excited."

"No, it's okay. You just caught me by surprise."

"Ohmygod, I'm really so sorry." I wrapped my hands tight around the steering wheel and drove past the turn off to the Harbour Chophouse and Birch Bay Burgers.

His hand lightly touched my arm in a gentle pat. "You were saying? Tell me about the weather."

Keeping my hands where I could see them, I inhaled to catch my breath and slow my words. "Well, we typically get very little snow but sometimes we'll get a big dumping, and when we do there's a snow hill not too far away with great sledding facilities – it's a not to be missed winter activity. However, we're mostly pretty tame, weather wise like Vancouver, but not quite as cloudy. In fact, our sunny days outshine our cloudy ones."

"That's a nice change. A lot of cloud of Vancouver, and it can wear on a person."

"A lot of go-go-go too. Here, not so much." As we approached downtown once again, I waved at a couple of moms pushing their strollers. "Everyone is much more relaxed. Shops close by supper, although some may stay open. The grocery mart is open until eight, so plan your trips wisely." I laughed. "But all restaurants and the bar and the pub are open late, so it's not like there's nothing to do. Oh, there's the school."

"All grades?"

I gave him a funny look because Cheshire Bay wasn't that small. "No. K to eight, if you can believe it. In the fall, the nine to twelves will be bussed to Stewart Surf."

"Not enough people?"

"There are only a few dozen in each grade, which is great, but by amalgamating, the kids would have more options, so it's really for the benefit of the students that it's happening."

"Why do I hear sadness in your voice?"

"Because, then Stewart Surf will keep them, and high schoolers with disposable income will spend there rather than here since they are already there. And they may get jobs there too. With parents picking them up, they may stay in Stewart Surf, and our shops and eateries may suffer."

"You make it sound like Cheshire Bay is dying."

"Not dying, no. Oh, here's the local pub – Amber's Ale. Has a great sand-side pub in the summer. Amber, she's the owner-operator, is the salt of the earth – you'll love her when you meet her. She's bubbly and warm, and people just feel relaxed around her, and tend to tell her all their problems."

He chuckled. "Is she one of your sisters?"

I narrowed my eyes, until I understood what he was getting at. "No."

"Is being bubbly a side effect of living here?"

"Maybe." A faint heat blossomed over my chest, which thankfully was covered by my blouse. "Did you know Cheshire Bay swells considerably in the summer?"

"Is that so?"

A broad smile stretched out my lips, and a smugness caused my shoulders to rock back and forth with pride. "A lot of people return here to stay in their beach homes. My friend Eric, the pilot who brought you here, he lives on a strip of beach homes that are often vacated come September long weekend but burst with life starting May long. You'll see. We call them the Summer Squad."

"Sounds interesting."

"It is. Francesca, my sister, she'sbeen waiting for one of the properties to go on the market so she can scoop it up and live on the beach year round, but they never list."

"And you would know."

"Yes, I would. Those homes," I pointed to the strip of a dozen houses, "they're passed down through the generations mostly." He leaned forward to listen to every syllable. "Winter is pretty quiet, relatively speaking, but the summer is busy. Lots to do. I can give you a list of the best public beaches, as well as a lot of hidden gems we don't share with the tourists."

"Why not?" His eyes narrowed.

"Because then they're not available for us, silly." I winked. "As much as I love this town, there are a few secrets within it I like to keep to myself."

"Is that so?"

"Yes. Oh, here we are." I pulled in front of the locked gate and parked the car, hopping out with my set of keys.

Zachary stood beside me at the lock.

Continuing with my tour guide attitude, I pointed to the ocean off to our left, not that he, or anyone, could miss it. "Those homes along the road there, those are mostly occupied by the summer squad. Behind the houses is a strip of the best sand in Cheshire Bay – pure beige sand, almost like flour."

"What are the other beaches made with? Aren't all beaches sandy?" A quizzical look dominated his handsome face.

I shifted on my heels as I tried a key in the lock. "Oh no. Here we have quite the variety; there's Glass Beach, Black Sand beach which is mostly black in colour and that's how it got his colourful name, but it's not as course as regular sand, and there's also Pebble Beach."

"All within this little town?"

"I know, right? You'll have to check them all out and tell me which is your favourite."

"Are you doing a survey?"

"Nope, just highly interested." I stared deep into his eyes, which upon closer inspection were actually two different colours, but not dramatically different.

The keys clattered out of my hand onto the asphalt.

Zachary bent down and grabbed them. "Which key is it?"

I tossed my gaze from his bright soulful eyes to the ring of keys. "Um, the long one I think."

He tried a couple until one clicked, and the lock popped open. Zachary loosened the rusty chain from one of the heavy iron gates, and pushed them both open, standing there as I inched the car forward.

Once the gate was closed, but not locked, we continued up the driveaway.

"So, the old Lowell place doesn't have a beach, but you can see how close he was to one, until, for reasons I can't remember, decades ago he sold a parcel of it to the town?" I shook my head and shrugged. I probably should've brushed up on that section of history especially since I was trying to sell the founding father's homestead.

The driveway was long, and it weaved its way to the left, where it rose high above the strip of beach houses and had the most impressive view of the ocean.

We both hopped out of the car and walked to the grassy edge. "Those are the beach homes of the summer squad, but we're high enough up to not have them block any sort of view."

"No, wow. This is amazing. The pictures never really did this justice."

It was hard to disagree – the view was magnificent. The sun was high overhead, but the waves in the ocean still glittered like diamonds in the light blue waters. It was breathtaking, and the fresh ocean scent was only masked by a fragrant spray of blossoming flowers.

"These are blooming a little late, but we did have a colder than average winter." I saw his raised brow. "But don't you worry. It's unusual. Most of the time, it's pretty mild. Very much like Vancouver."

"But better?" A smirk appeared.

"Much better." I tipped my chin down and fought against the rush of feel-good vibes coursing through my veins.

"Tell me about this land." Zachary stepped a little closer and the scent rolling off him in the breeze was enough to make me weak in the knees.

I listed all the details, anything and everything I could think of, and even reiterated the minute information in the inspection report. He stood stoically, hands in his pockets, head tipped to the side, listening to it all. I've been the centre of attention several times before, but this was more. It was captivating.

"Is that all?" He laughed as I finished my monologue.

I tapped my finger on my chin and sent my view away from his charming face to a flock of seagulls circling nearby. "Yeah, I do believe so. Is there anything I missed that you didn't get an answer to?"

"No, you're very thorough."

"Thank you, it's part of the job." And it was. Any relator worth her money made damn sure she knew the ins and out of every listing.

He briefly spun away from me, admiring the ocean view, and turned to the house. "It's perfect. I'll take it."

What? He hadn't even seen the inside yet.

"Are you sure? I can give you a tour?" I held up the house key. This was a first.

"Won't be necessary, Miss MacDonald. I've seen the inside via the pictures and read the inspectors report. You sealed the deal with your grand tour of the area. You should be the spokesmodel for Cheshire Bay and area, you do a fantastic job."

I swallowed. "Thank you."

"Do you have the papers with you?"

Chapter Three

I n the kitchen, where the double-paned sink window overlooks the glittering Pacific, Zachary signed the papers with gusto. Once I triple checked nothing was amiss, I stuck the papers into my portfolio.

"Standard procedure. Once we get it all approved, and the bank agrees—"

"There won't be any issues from the bank, I promise." He crossed his heart with his fingers. "But I know the steps that happen next."

"Not your first home purchase?"

"Not by a long shot." He beamed. "Although this is my first purchase here, if that makes you feel better." He handed back my pen, his fingers grazing mine for a fraction of a second longer than normal.

I rolled my gaze up from his hand to his hooded eyes, my pounding heartbeat rendering me utterly speechless.

"Is there anything else you need, Miss MacDonald?"

Slowly, I shook my head, and my satiny hair hung over my shoulders. "No. Not at all. I think we're good. I'll drive you back to your car." I snapped my fingers, pointing at him. "Oh wait, you didn't drive to the bookstore, did you? Where are you staying?"

"At the Bay Western." From his back pocket, he pulled out the old-style blue plastic keychain formed in the shape of the room number; it dangled off a beaded chrome chain. It seriously aged the place and had zero in the charm department. "My suitcase is already there."

"Oh. Well then. I can drop you off."

"I wouldn't want to take up anymore of your time. You've been an endearing tour guide and representative for your town."

"Honestly, I wouldn't mind. I'm heading to the courthouse anyway." Besides, I didn't want to leave his presence just yet. There was something about him I found myself yearning to learn more about.

"If you don't mind, then, I'd love to take you up on that offer. I need to see the mayor about a few permits and such myself." He moved toward the front door.

"Oh, be sure to take her a maple macchiato from Java & Lattes; it's her favourite. It might not sway her decision about what you need, but it'll put you in her good books."

Tonya Vasquez, our mayor for the last two terms, had a serious sweet tooth.

"And what is your favourite?"

"Huh?" I closed and locked the door of the Lowell place.

"Your favourite? From Java & Lattes?"

"Chai. A vanilla chai." I didn't even hesitate. Hands down. If my aunt made them, I'd never have a reason to visit the coffee shop.

"Great choice. You can never go wrong with something spicy." His gaze roamed from my eyes and settled on my lips for a heartbeat, before returning to look over my shoulder. "This really is a remarkable view."

"One of the best in Cheshire Bay. Guess that's why Mr. Lowell stayed here for so long. Would be hard to not enjoy this scenery."

But I wasn't looking at the ocean, I was checking out the barest hint of a five o'clock shadow forming along his strong jawline, and the nape of his neck where it was easy to see he'd recently had a haircut – his hairline was perfectly trimmed. His skin was a touch golden, not like the kind from hours in the sun, but more of a natural colour, or perhaps he tanned in the winter months or jetted to far away places for a bit of a reprieve.

"What do you think?" He patted my arm.

"Sorry, what was that?"

"What's got you so deep in thought?"

"Honestly, I was just wondering if you travelled to exotic locales, and how if you did, you might find that now you won't have to, and it would be easier on your stomach if you didn't need to travel. Cheshire Bay has everything you'll ever need." I popped a smile onto my face.

"You never travel away from here?"

"Not for ocean settings. I have travelled to New York, but it only makes me yearn desperately for coming home. It's too people-y and way too crowded. I didn't last very long before I was practically begging to come home." Homesickness was a real thing as far as I was concerned.

"Totally a small-town gal, eh?"

"All the way."

A twinkle appeared in his eyes, but he jutted his chin toward the car. "Shall we go?"

"Oh, yes. I should think you'd like to get things settled as quickly as possible."

"It's true. I don't like to dawdle." He walked beside me to the car and waited until I slipped behind the wheel before walking to his side. "Can I ask you something?"

I swallowed as I started the engine, putting the car into gear – the driveway was wide enough to not need to resort to a five-point turn. "Of course. If you're wanting information on any sporting teams, the only one we sort of have is a curling team. One of our residents though is moving to Alberta because her team is doing so well. Rumour has it, there could be an Olympic spot in their future."

"That's pretty amazing, really, but I'm not interested in sports."

I gasped. "Really? Not even hockey?"

"Especially hockey. I have better things to do than watch a bunch of over-waning egos push each other around the ice and occasionally score once in a while."

"Wow, tell me how you really feel." I laughed. Whereas I could take it or leave it, Ashley was a diehard fan, and lived and breathed hockey. "What did you want to know that I haven't already covered?" I thought I'd gone over everything, but clearly I'd missed something.

"Is there a special someone in your life?"

My lips remained firmly together, and my gaze narrowed slightly, just like the gaps in my breaths. I reminded myself he probably does this with everyone.

"Because I'd like to ask you out to dinner, but," he grimaced, "if you're already spoken for, then I don't need your boyfriend to come and beat me up." He twisted in his seat and waited for my answer.

Going out for a dinner date would be fun, and a long time

coming, however, I knew at least this would be a temporary thing. He was only here for a couple of days, at least until he moved.

He gave his attention to the gate we were approaching. "That's okay. Forget I asked."

"No, it's not that. It's just…" What were the words I was searching for? "It's.. Well… Yes, I'd love that." An involuntary smile burst free from my lips. "Yes, let's go out for dinner. I like dinner."

"Excellent." He pushed his shoulders into the seat, relief breezing out between his perfect lips. "Do you like steak for dinner?"

"I do."

"You mentioned the Chophouse has great steaks?"

"The best."

"Let's test out that theory." He winked, and the seams on my panties dissolved slightly. Damn, he was good.

"You'll see I'm correct." My words were borderline breathless. Seriously, I needed to get a grip on myself and check my heart at the door.

"I love your optimism."

We took an abbreviated trip back to A Whole New World, where I parked alongside the bookstore.

"The mayor's office is just down Main Street, above Daisy's Delights. They're on the north side of street."

"Thank you, Mia." He exited the car, but before he got both feet on the sidewalk, he faced me. "Normally, I would pick you up and drive *you* around, so I feel really weird asking if you'd meet me at the Chophouse."

"Nothing weird about that."

He shrugged. "Standard practice right? Safer to meet a guy someplace."

"Maybe." I handed him his nearly empty water bottle. "Why don't I pick you up from the hotel? And we can go from there?"

He shook his head and patted his shirt pocket. "Actually, if you don't mind, I'm going to walk the trails and check this place out, see what Cheshire Bay is all about."

"You'll love it." And deep down, I truly hoped he did. Small towns, especially ours, were so different than a big city.

"Meet you there for seven-thirty?"

"Works for me." I blushed a smile as he stood on the sidewalk.

"Enjoy your afternoon."

"You too."

He closed the door.

I rolled down my window. "Don't forget the maple macchiato. Java & Lattes, it's on the corner."

Sending a quick finger gun my way, he said, "Thanks for the reminder."

I arrived at Harbour Chophouse at exactly seven-thirty, and the place was a beehive of activity, including the wait area. Thankfully, I had the smarts to call in a favour and book us a table for two, on the patio facing the ocean. I wanted to show Zachary just how amazing everything in Cheshire Bay was.

I'd just announced to the hostess I was here when I spotted him sauntering in from the double doors. He'd changed, like me, and was dressed in a crisp dark blue shirt, with a purple tie, dark pants, and a sport jacket. He looked magnificent. Whereas he dressed up, I'd dressed down – slightly. A full-length maxi dress with a cute empire waist, wrapped under a handmade cardigan that Ashley had called a shawl, even though those were two different items.

As Zachary approached, a spicy scent, reminiscent of something my dad used to wear years ago, like Old Spice, but not quite. It wasn't overpowering, but I did notice how one of the ladies in the wait area gave him a solid once over as he passed by.

"Good evening, Zachary." I extended my hand. We were only on a business date, right? Or was it more?

He enclosed my hand with his, never removing his focus from me, and moved in to drop a kiss on my cheek. "Good evening, Mia. You look stunning."

Oh yeah, this was no business date, and the sudden thundering of my pulse confirmed that.

"Thank you." I had taken a few extra minutes to make sure my hair was poker straight and polished, so there was a sheen to the strands. I preferred the straight over my natural curls, to me I looked more professional. Glad to hear it was worth the trouble. "They were just about to take me to our table."

"Mia?" the hostess called out. "Right this way, please."

We followed her through the busy dining room, and out the glass doors onto a heated patio. She stopped in front of a quaint table for two, nestled off to the side with little foot traffic to bother us. Plus, the view was magnificent.

"This okay?" She asked me in particular.

"Perfect." I sat and crossed my legs with a quick shiver, grateful I chose a longer dress as the air had a bit of a nip in it.

Zachary sat too and pointed to the outdoor heater. "Is it possible to turn the heat up a little?"

"Absolutely, sir." She handed us each a leather-bound menu, took our drink order, and left us alone after adjusting the heat.

A wave of warmth breezed over me.

"So… what do you think of the view?" I tipped my head to the ocean.

Below the deck, the lights bathed the ocean and every so often a spray of water crested the top of the water, highlighting the splash.

"Amazing." He turned his focus back to me.

"The best restaurant view in all the bay area, maybe even on the whole island." Smugness filled my tone, but I kept it on the playful side.

"Do you always talk about this town?"

"Not always." I fiddled with the cloth napkin and draped it over my lap.

"Let's change the parameters, shall we?" He inched his chair closer to mine. "Tonight, I'm not a client purchasing a property, and you're not the agent trying to sell me on it. You're Mia and I'm Zachary, and we're two people out to enjoy the other's company."

I chuckled, tipping my head back slightly. "Thank you for clarifying how a date works. I know it's been sometime since I've done this, and I had wondered if things had changed."

His smile faded slightly. "Been awhile?"

"A couple of months." I shrugged. "But it's all good. First dates happen enough, but since breaking up with my fiancé, nothing much beyond a second date occurs."

"You were engaged before?"

Throwing my focus out to the ocean, and the occasional light splashing in the distance from the lighthouse, I inhaled. "I don't talk about it. It's in the past, and in the words of Doc Brown, *my future isn't written yet, so make it a good one.*"

The server set down our drinks and took our food order

before leaving us alone again.

"Fair enough. No talks about the past, and minimal," he held up a finger, "talk about this town. You've already helped convince me it's a must-see."

"So, tonight there is no conversation around the property? I can't even ask you about what kind of place you have back in Vancouver?" I took a sip of my Negroni. It was perfect; my own didn't have quite the same zest.

"Well..." Zachary lifted his chilled mug of draft. "I have no qualms about that."

"Great." I leaned a little closer, running my finger over the lip of my glass. "So, tell me, what do you do back home?"

"Business deals, nothing very exciting, but it does take me to some interesting locations."

"Oooh, like where?"

"I've made some deals in Europe, but most of the deals are in North and South America, with a greater focus on North American deals." He tipped a bit of the beer back. "But it's work. Not very interesting. What about you? You've always been a realtor?"

"Yep." I bobbed my finger into my drink, and when it was sufficiently wet, I popped it into my mouth and sucked the citrusy taste off. "I mainly focus on Cheshire Bay, but I've sold places in Stewart Surf on occasion."

"Is Stewart Surf nice?"

I tipped my head to the side. "Isn't that a leading question? I thought all conversations about the area were off the table?"

"Ten points to you. I guess I'll just check it out myself." His eyes sparkled with the challenge. "Or perhaps, if I'm not being too forward, maybe on our second date you can give me a tour?"

"Perhaps, assuming there's a second date." I took in this handsome man sitting beside me, knowing full well if he asked me out again, I'd say yes before the question was fully asked. "You know I have to ask, mainly because it's unusual..." I tucked my right foot behind my left ankle and leaned forward on my arms.

"Are you referring to my two different coloured eyes?" He bridged the already narrow distance between us and tipped his head up to just catch the overhead lights.

His eyes were amazing, but they weren't all that different - one was a greenish brown but more on the greenish side and the other was a light brown, like melted milk chocolate. It wasn't like one was bright blue and the other deep brown, his were subtle, and you really had to stare, like I was doing.

I cleared my throat and tossed my gaze over to the ocean. "Well, that's something unusual for sure, but that wasn't what I was going to inquire about."

"Oh?" He pulled back just a bit and a swirl of cool air raced in. It was warmer when he was closer, like it was trapping the heat between us.

"Your last name. Not many men have a hyphenated last name."

"They don't, and I wish I had a fun story to go with it. Basically, it was a fight between my parents, as both wanted their last names on my birth certificate."

"So, whose name is first? Who won that battle?"

"My dad. He figured when I got older I'd drop the second name." He chuckled and took another sip of his beer. "The only problem comes when I get married again. If my wife wants my last name, then it's easy, still long, but easy, however, what if she doesn't want my two names?"

"Did your ex-wife have both of yours?"

He shook his head and cleared his throat. "No, she kept hers, which led to an interesting question. What about our kids? What last name goes with them? A kid with four names, one first name and three hyphenated last names is a mouthful."

"Yeah, that would be a problem. Something to cross when you get there, I guess. Or a conversation for a fourth or fifth date." Although, I just couldn't keep my mouth shut. "But what you could do, and this is funny, only because as a person with a legally hyphenated last name."

"Really?"

"Oh yeah. My adopted family, they are all Normandys, but I was born a MacDonald. My adoptive parents wanted to keep part of my heritage, so they hyphenated my name, but business wise, it's too long, so I just use MacDonald, and they're okay with that."

"Interesting." He nodded, shifting in his seat. "And what would you do with your future children's last names?"

"Well," I fought a smile desperate to poke through with my own little inside joke. "Each child gets a different last name. The boy would have Normandy, to carry on that lineage as a thank you to my adoptive family, and MacDonald would go to my daughter. You could do the same with your kids – your dad's name, then your mom's, then the wife's."

"Again, problematic."

"Because? Three kids aren't too many." I was the middle child of five, so three would be the sweet spot. Everyone fit in one vehicle *comfortably*, and each had their own room – no bunking up.

"It is for me. I only want two." He held up his hand, just in case I couldn't remember what the number two looked like.

I covered his hand and pushed it back to the table. "I'll

pretend I didn't just see that." I shook my head in mock. "Was it tough growing up an only child?"

He shrugged, and it briefly opened a gap between his neck and collar, allowing me a quick peek inside. There was a bit of chest hair visible. Rawr.

"There was no sharing of toys, no one to steal my clothes, or be the last one to get a hot shower, so it wasn't that bad."

"You grew up in my house, eh?" I laughed because that's exactly what it was like. My sisters stole my clothes, or I'd borrow theirs, and if you were the last for a shower, you ended up having a quick one - unless you enjoyed cold showers. Which I never did.

"But it was lonely. No one to play with, and my parents just didn't have time. They enrolled me in everything, from piano lessons to an eight-week soccer season to tutoring, even though I was a B+ student."

The smile faded from his face, and I mirrored it, touching his arm. "That must've been rough."

"Wasn't too bad. As I got older, I did what I wanted, and no one cared."

"Lucky you, although, by the time I came along, no one much cared either. You'd be surprised at the amount of shit we got away with, especially since Erin and Adam had broken in my parents, and they were immune to the shenanigans from the rest of us."

Ah the memories. Some sweet, some not so much.

"You too?" He pulled back when our server appeared with our steaming and savoury steaks with a giant potato with all the fixings. "If my parents knew the things I did, they'd probably disown me."

"Ooh, like what?" The pull for a bit of a bad boy lit the fires deep inside. My first crush had been an honest to God true bad boy, and my heart never fully recovered. "Illegal?"

"No, never." He said the two words so fast, they blended together. "More like I coloured outside the lines, but not too bad. Mostly just missing curfew on occasion, until they took my car away."

"See, your parents did care." I cut into my steak, and a river of pink juices flowed out – perfection.

"No. They cared about their image. A kid bucking the rules wasn't ideal, so I had to tow the line."

"Moved out early I take it?" I pegged him moving out the moment he walked across the stage to collect his high school diploma.

"Eighteen."

I was right. "How did you manage college?"

"I have great skills." He cocked an eyebrow, and I nearly melted. "My time management priorities are A+."

"That's a good one to have." I slipped a piece of steak off my fork and into my mouth. The steak was so flavourful, I moaned. "Damn. See? They know how to make a steak here. Try yours."

He did, and a giant head nod and satisfactory smile lit up his whole face.

"You know, this place was establish—"

His right eyebrow nearly joined his hairline.

"You know what, it's not important."

"That's the ticket." His foot bumped against mine. "However, I would like your thoughts on where one goes for a second date?"

Lord help me, a second date? It had been a long time since I'd had one of those – my verbal diarrhea tended to send them running.

"When will you be back?"

"A couple of weeks at least."

"The weather will be better, and I have a few places in mind. What's your adventure level like?"

Chapter Four

itting with Zachary Newton-Garcia and enjoying the best meal I've shared with a guy in a long time, was high on my list of pleasurable activities I'd like to do again. A second date would definitely be in order and be most welcomed.

He was a perfect gentleman, and even though I insisted, repeatedly, he paid for the bill and walked me to my car.

"Miss Mia, I must tell you, this has been the best night I've ever had in Cheshire Bay."

"You've had others?"

"Nope." A smirk appeared.

"So how can it be the best then?"

"Because meeting you, seeing this town, it's changed my perspective on things. Plus, the bar is set so high, I'm not sure how each day will surpass this."

"You need to get out more."

"I'm serious." He stood impossibly close, his gaze roaming around my face, yet occasionally it focused on my lips.

Little butterflies took flight in my gut, and I loved the sensation. "When you move here, you'll see. There's no place else

I'd rather be."

The breeze picked up and rustled through the nearby trees, and a shiver shook my body. It was late spring, so the evenings were more on the crisp side.

He brushed a strand of hair from my cheeks. "Would you care to join me for a nightcap?"

Every part of me did; from the tips of my hair floating in the wind, to my core which was warming faster than a summer's day at Hardy Beach, to the toes I hoped he had the power to curl. But I couldn't. I shouldn't.

I sighed. "I want to, but I can't."

"Oh." His hands fell to his sides. "Okay."

"It's not you, and it's not that I don't want to, I'm just…Well," How to put it so it didn't sound crazy, and not cliché? "It's me. I'm still trying to navigate things, and it's been a while. I'm still trying to figure out what won't destroy me when it ends."

"I see. You hate tragic endings?"

Rather than watch a grimace slowly leak its way onto his face, I focused on the main doors of Harbour Chophouse. "We had plans to get married, and things just didn't go that way. After a few years together, we were different people with different goals. And now, I'm trying to get back on the horse, but it's difficult."

"You'd rather just pet the horse than ride it?" It was said so sweetly, and the gentle way he grazed his fingers across my cheek, had my heart skipping a beat and my mind kicking it back into a regular rhythm, along with the words *just do it. Say yes. Go with him.*

I stared into his face, into the warm eyes that held sincerity. "For now."

"I can respect that."

DREAMERS IN CHESHIRE BAY

And I believed him, as nothing in my body set off warnings. Except of my apparent stupidity in not following this man back to his motel room and showing him a good time.

"Thank you," I said, willing my heart to calm itself down. "For today, and buying the Lowell place, to dinner tonight. I had a great time."

"Me too."

I stood there, wavering back and forth on my feet. "See you around?"

"Oh, I have a feeling we'll bump into each other again. Besides, you did suggest there may be a second date."

"Yes, I did. When we see each other again, we can set it up."

"Deal."

"Goodnight, Zachary."

"Goodnight, Mia." My heart screamed at me all the way to my car, and my mind, usually the most logical in these situations, linked hands with my heart and joined in the adamant belittling. A couple of weeks wasn't too long to wait, was it?

I closed the lid on my laptop with a satisfied sigh. The paperwork was all complete on the Lowell place, easy as slicing pie. Zachary's legal support was top notch, as was his bank since it was a done deal. I could hand over the keys without any hesitation.

Walking in from the back patio of Amber's Ale, I set my empty glass down on the bar.

"Thanks, Amber."

"You know, it looks bad when my customers bring in their dirty dishes." She tossed a white barkeep towel over her shoulder.

"Just saving you a trip outside. There's a storm brewing,

and I was the last one out there."

"Ugh, I hate storms."

"Me too." Storms scared the crap out of me. The only place I felt comfortable enduring them was at home with all the lights on and multiple bass heavy songs blaring on the radio.

"Shall I add the coffee and Bailey's to your tab?" She grabbed the glass and set it into the bussing tray, glancing at me through the reflection in the mirror.

"Actually, let's pay the tab off."

"Early this month."

Not everyone was allowed to run a monthly tab, but Amber had let me. She was one of my first clients; I had sold her the bar and the apartment above which she lived in.

Now, with the sale of the Lowell place, I suddenly had a huge influx of cash. Or at least had it coming, so I may as well clear up my debts.

Punching the screen of her tablet, Amber quickly pulled up the amount owing, and showed me, scrolling through the list.

"Looks good." I waited as the numbers beeped on the point-of-sale machine until she handed it to me. Even though I always left a cash tip behind every time I was in, I added a nice twenty percent to the total. I turned the handheld device back to her.

"Thanks, Mia." She ripped off the piece of paper, folded it, and handed it over. "There's a new guy in town, eh?"

I turned in the direction of her stare.

Lo and behold, Mr. Zachary Newton-Garcia was tucked into the corner by the jukebox, madly typing away, an unmistakeable white ear pod visible.

"Oh, him? That's Zachary. He'll be moving here. Just bought the old Lowell place."

"It's not just going to sit vacant anymore?"

"Nope. The family finally decided to let it go. Cleaned it out and listed it." Through the mirrored reflection, I watched intently as he typed, his perfect lips moving in conversation.

"About time it finally sold." She nodded and wiped an invisible speck from the bar counter. "Anyway, thanks for popping in. See you next week?"

"Of course." I bid her adieu and walked over to Zachary, putting a little spring into my steps.

"Thanks, I'll touch base tomorrow when I'm in the office," he said, and then looked up as I approached, a smile a mile wide plastered from ear to ear. "Well, good morning, Mia. It's still morning, right?" He glanced at his watch, a gold Rolex, or at least it looked like it.

"It's still morning."

"Please, have a seat." He stood and pulled out a chair for me. "I was just finishing up with my business partner."

I sat in the offered chair, tucking my laptop bag at my feet. "Hope all is good?"

"Things are great." There was a lightness in his voice that complimented his words.

"You're sounding better. Must be all that fresh ocean air."

A light chuckle danced around my ears. "Perhaps." He drew it out into two long syllables. "Or... It might be because I saw an herbalist, that one tucked upstairs on Second Ave above the pita place, and she concocted some kind of tincture that worked amazingly well."

"You didn't see Dr. Singh?"

"Nah. Don't get me wrong, I'm all for western medicine, but sometimes, thinking outside the box works too, and eastern medicine has that."

I wasn't sure I'd believe anything an herbalist would say, but it wasn't my body, so I kept my lips sealed and moved on. "How was your first overnight?"

He leaned closer, although there were only a handful of people in the pub. "A little lonely, if I'm honest."

My heart pitter patted as I breathed him in, all fresh cologne, a hint of coffee breath, and dare I say cinnamon too? "I do appreciate the truth. It's lacking these days, but I'm not sorry you were alone. Not completely anyway."

Oh hell, I was so hot and bothered last night when I went home, I had a little solo time in the tub. Should've just accepted his offer, it would've been more pleasurable.

He took the bait, briefly, his mouth opening a smidge as if to speak, but it closed. After a sharp inhale, he spoke again. "But that motel bed? Good grief. I think the floor may have been more comfortable. Someone needs to buy it and give it a serious overhaul. I'm not even sure it's up to code."

I shrugged. "I'm sure the mayor wouldn't approve it for licensing each year if it was that shabby."

He leaned back in the wooden chair, a lopsided grin forming. "Maybe someone gave her one of her favourite drinks and she signed on the dotted lines without looking?"

"Why, Zachary, are you throwing my own words back at me?"

"Maybe." The creases around his eyes deepened as the left side of his smile pushed his cheeks nice and high. Seeing it, sent a wave of pleasure through my body. "I'm off to see her again this afternoon."

"Ah yes. I just got the good word on the sale. Congrats. I can meet you at your house to officially hand over the keys since I don't have them. What time works best for you?"

He tipped his head back and voiced his itinerary. "I can meet you there for three?"

"Three works." It gave me time to freshen up and dabble on a little of my favourite perfume. Have you booked your movers yet?"

He ran his hands through his dark hair. "It's on my list of things to do, but it's way at the bottom."

"Oh." Not sure why I was suddenly so sad; he'd gotten approval from legal and financial. Figured he'd be moving here in no time flat. "Do you have a date in mind?"

"For possession? Or for tonight?"

I certainly wouldn't refuse a second offer of possessing me. Well, damn. I swallowed, wondering if he could see the telltale beat of my heart in my neck? "Moving here."

"I'll get all those details worked out when I go home tomorrow."

"How long will you be there?" Was it wrong to want him back here as soon as possible?

"I have a pile of work to do, but a couple of weeks and I'll be returning?" He lifted a finger to pause and tapped his phone. "Just a sec. Hey, William. Can you give me fifteen minutes? I'll call you right back."

"Sorry, I should let you go." I stood and picked up my bag, patting him on the shoulder like we were old friends. "See you at your new place for three?"

He rose and stood impossibly close. "Yes. Can we move up our second date to tonight? There's a place I want to check out, and I need a good tour guide to help me."

OMG. A second date. Today. Tonight.

Reminding myself to breathe, because If I didn't get control of myself, and fast, I'd be the laughingstock of Cheshire

Bay with my quick, breathless response. Keeping my tone light and casual, I slowly nodded. "Sure. I'll bring a change of shoes."

I looked down to my high heeled feet.

"Bring a change of clothes, too, or come in more comfortable clothing."

"What is it you have in mind, Mr. Newton-Garcia?" Well, damn. That came out more sensual than I wanted, and I gave my desperate brain a mental swift kick.

"All in good time." A panty-melting wink came my way. "Can I walk you out to your car?"

"I think I can manage it, but it's sweet of you to ask." I gave him a quick wave. "See you at three."

"Looking forward to it."

I hopped in my car and raced home, wondering what to wear on a second date. What exactly did Zachary have in mind? Was it the same as me?

Chapter Five

After an hour of painstaking deliberation, I narrowed down my choice to black leggings and an oversized cable knit sweater. They paired nicely with my chunky heeled black boots, so I was ready for anything. I even put on my favourite matched set of purple satin underthings; a demi-cup bra and a g-string. Just in case. There was something about Zachary that was driving my carnal pleasure system off the charts. For some reason, I just couldn't wait to see him again, and it was unnerving.

While waiting at the gates of the Lowell place, which should now be renamed to the Newton-Garcia place, I opened the fresh box of condoms, tucked one into my legging pocket and stowed the rest under the seat. Nothing wrong with being safe, nor prepared. Not having had a second date in years, I wasn't sure how the afternoon would go. Laughing, I knew I was ready for anything.

Mr. Sweet and Gorgeous arrived just before three and stepped out of the taxi carrying two paper bags of groceries.

"Well, guess you're moving in now." I chuckled gently, took a bag from his arm, and offered him the keys. "These are now yours, and you should have the honour of unlocking your gate and your house."

"Why, thank you." He juggled the other bag in one arm, and the lock with his free hand, eventually releasing the chain. "Welcome. Won't you join me for a little housewarming?" The bag rustled as he hoisted it up on his hip.

"It would be my pleasure."

Setting the bags on the floor of my backseat, we left the gate open, and drove up the winding driveway, parking near the door.

"Looks like there's going to be some rain tonight." Zachary gazed out over the darkening ocean. "I love the rain – the fresh scent, how it washes everything away."

"It's supposed to be a storm, but nothing's happened yet."

"I can't wait."

I set the bag on the step by the door and took Zachary's to free his hands. "I can."

"Not a fan of storms, or just the rain?"

"Storms." A shudder rippled through me.

"What is it you don't like?" He flipped between the keys.

"It's the larger one." I watched as he popped that into the lock and twisted. "I can mostly handle the rumbles, but I don't like the crackers and definitely don't like the flashes."

"So, I guess my plan for watching it roll in, on my new deck, is out of the question?"

"For me, yeah, but you go right ahead."

He opened the door, ushered me in, and I walked into the empty house, setting the bags on the long island in the kitchen. From within the paper bag, he pulled out a wine bottle and a sleeve of a dozen plastic wine glasses.

"Was the best I could find on short notice." He twisted the

golden cap off and poured two glasses of red, handing one to me. "Thank you for showing me this place. It's perfect."

"Thank you for buying it. Your move in gift comes in a couple of weeks."

"Ooh, what did you get?"

"You'll see." I took the glass and lifted it. "But it's homemade. My sister Erin, she makes the most incredible painted wood products, and she's working on something."

"Wow. Well, thank you in advance." He lifted his wine.

Our plastic glasses touched, as did our fingers.

He shot his back, and I did the same; the glasses didn't hold much. Would take a half dozen each to empty the bottle, not like my 12oz glass at home.

After the third glass though, I was starting to feel a slight buzz, and I took in the label on the bottle. It was high end, very high end, not likely from someplace local, but maybe as I wasn't a frequent visitor to the liquor store, and the alcohol content matched. Since I hadn't eaten since breakfast, it explained the gentle intoxication I was feeling.

"So, I'm assuming you got everything handled with the mayor? Did you take her a special drink?"

"No drink needed; I just used my magnetic charming personality." He put one foot forward and raked a hand through his hair all the while posing like a model on the runaway.

I nearly burst out laughing. "Oh really? And that worked?" I waved a hand up and down his body. "She's a married woman."

"And very set in her ways." Breaking character, he shook his head playfully as a smirk curled the left side of his plump lips. He sauntered closer, removing much of the space between us. "But I'm not interested in her, so no, it didn't work because I didn't try."

"Oh?" My gaze roamed his face, from his two different coloured eyes, over his prominent cheekbones, to the dimple residing just under his bottom lip.

"I am interested in you."

"So, this is definitely a second date?" I swallowed. I'd hoped he'd been interested, but it was so bold and daring to truly admit it to myself.

He brushed his hand along my cheeks and tucked my poker-straight hair behind my ear. "Yes."

"And how do I know that you're just not playing me? To see if I'm just a local attraction?"

"Because I know you're not. Reading people is a skill I've had all my life, and I just get a solid sense of who they are in a very short time. You're easy to read."

A small pea-sized lump formed in the back of my throat; now I was worried he thought less of me.

"What's with that face? It's not bad. I love how you get so excited by your hometown. It really is a remarkable place and having lived in a big city all my life, I just can't wrap my head around this place. Everyone already knows who I am. How is that possible?"

"Small town network, or the STN for now. The gossip mill is crazy high here. There's even a gossip column in our weekly newspaper. You'll be top news in Sunday's edition."

He shook his head. "Really? How old school is that gossip column?"

"It's actually pretty neat. Most of it is fun stuff, like Old Man Veer was caught sweeping the sidewalks for his neighbours. It's mostly harmless."

"That's… really kind of cool."

"Occasional though, the darker rumours swirl, but that's

mostly through the STN. There's even a rumour that one of the summer squad kids has moved back into her old summer place on the strip. Actually, just below here. She was a bad ass, although I never knew her personally, but allegedly she was responsible for another kid's death. The town isn't taking it too well that she's back."

"She's a murderer?" His eyes grew in size.

"No," I said, shaking my head, "I don't think so. The kid's death was accidental, but somehow, she's involved."

"Yikes."

"It was years ago. But she's back, that's all I know, like fresh. A couple of days, if that. If you want all the gossip, sit in Amber's pub, and only pretend to have your ear pod on. I'm sure most of the rumours start there."

"Is Amber the gossip queen?"

"Not at all. She tries to squash it pretty quickly, but the old ones who hang out in there, they're part of the STN. Probably heard your conversation today and started sharing the news when they walked the town."

Zachary paled slightly and stepped back. "God, I hope not. I was doing some business deals."

I glanced around the open concept home. "Well, now that you have the keys to your place, I'd suggest you do them here. Use the kitchen counter until your furniture arrives."

Releasing a long breath, he rocked on his feet and crossed his fingers. "Well, my business is done for the day, and I'm leaving in the morning, so I should be good."

"Now that you've taken possession, when are you coming back?" I really wished I'd kept the hint of whine from my tone, but I didn't want him to be gone for long. For the weekend, maybe, but I'd hoped a week tops.

"No date booked yet, but you'll be the first to know."

"I like being first." I moved closer, and the bolder part of me reached for his hand, threading my fingers through his. "But I don't want to be last."

"I don't think it would ever be possible to put you last."

I snorted.

"Is that what your fiancé did? Put you last?"

"Yes, and no. We'd been together for a long time, since high school, and after he popped the question a few years into our relationship, we just started drifting apart. It wasn't too long until we both noticed it too. He'd come home from work, and I wasn't jump-into-his-arms excited to see him."

"That fades though, in any relationship."

I shrugged. "Maybe. But if I had a late evening showing, he wasn't excited to see me either, and it's not that we hated the other, we just lost our zest. We'd become a habit, a quick kiss before bed, a brief goodbye as we parted. Like two ships in a harbour passing by. Nothing exciting."

"And you broke up because of it?"

"Yeah." I gave him a curious look. "The passion was gone, and when we honestly looked back on it, it was never there, not really. We seemed to function better, and happier, when we were apart."

"How long were you together?"

"Eight years."

His eyes widened and his jaw dropped. "Wow, that would be hard to walk away from."

"We've been separated for almost a year now. He's getting married in the fall. She's a wonderful lady, the town vet. I'm happy for them." And I was. Someday I'd find the one who put more than just a brief spark in me, someone I was passionate

53

about, who consumed me completely.

"Really?" He tipped his head to the side and studied me. "If that's true, then wow. You're a better person than I am."

"There's no point in holding a grudge. Life's too short."

"You are amazing." He brushed a hand over my cheek.

"Thanks, I try." The expression he gave me caused a rush of heat to swim across my chest, and although my cheeks felt like the temperature was growing, I hoped it wasn't visible. "Do you want to take this out on the deck?" I pointed to the wine and our cheap, plastic glasses.

"Sure." He broke his connection with me and stepped over to the bag where he dug inside and pulled out a platter of meat, cheese, and fruit. "Finger food. Figured a light snack was the right call before I require your help in locating this place I really want to check out tonight. Then, after we tour it, I can buy you a proper meal."

"What place are you wanting to find?"

He beamed brighter than the sun. "Apparently, my real estate agent mentioned there's a suspension bridge around here, and yet I can't seem to find it on any map?"

"Oh yes, that. Just off the highway. It's kind of a blink and you miss the turn, and it's not very well advertised, mostly just a local hidden gem. You need to walk through this thick forest of evergreens, which smell amazing this time of year and in the fall, and then you'll see the bridge. It spans across this gorgeous ravine of trees and a teeny, tiny creek. On the other side, you can follow the path to this amazing lookout." I blushed and looked down at my feet. "Sorry, rambling again."

"And I love it. Please don't ever change that." He grabbed the trays of finger food and guided me to the patio doors. "Can you hold?" Before I could answer, he dumped the trays in my hands and pulled open the french doors to an amazing seascape. "Is that lookout better than this?"

It had been a while since I'd been to the suspension bridge lookout point, but... I playfully shrugged, but in all honesty, nothing beat it. I couldn't imagine walking out to this every single day. "Maybe. It's a little more private. Here, if you get too close to the edge of the deck, you can see the strip of houses below."

"Then let's not get too close, shall we?" He set the trays on the wooden patio table the former owners had left behind and opened the lid to the storage box at the far end. "Blankets." He tossed them onto the deck once he removed them from the protective plastic bag. "They didn't leave chairs, but at least they left huge pillows."

The three pillows looked like they fit into one of those rattan chairs. They were plush, wide, and super comfortable.

We tossed two together for extra thickness, and huddled on one, stretching out our legs. It didn't even bother me how we were sharing the same pillow; I rather enjoyed being in the same immediate space with him.

It was the most natural feeling in the world. I didn't feel weird, or rushed, or out of place, but I wanted to push things and see how far I could take them. I squeezed his hand tight.

Our fingers laced together.

"Yep, this is one amazing view. Can't see the houses below. Totally private." He gazed out to the darkening ocean skies and then his focus turned to me. "Yes, truly a breathtaking view."

I stared into his handsome face, as a deep throbbing sensation rocked my core. The expression was all panty melting and heady, and my breath hitched in my throat seeing his eyes darken the longer he looked at me.

"You're beautiful."

"You're pretty handsome yourself." I flipped over onto my knees and inched closer, but in a fraction of a heartbeat, with zero hesitation, I'd cupped his whiskery face and brushed my lips over his.

"Damn," he said, pulling back just a touch to make strong eye contact.

"Too fast?" I grimaced.

"No, you just caught me by surprise. I thought you wanted to go slow?"

"To hell with it. Life's too short." I kissed him again and straddled his legs.

"Agreed." His hands wrapped around my back and held me tight as our lips first brushed lightly, teasingly, until a deep firm touch was desired. And needed.

I parted my lips, allowing him in, and our tongues danced and connected in ways that did more than just spark an ember – it sent a raging inferno through my soul.

He tugged my sweater over my head, the cool ocean breeze giving life to the goosebumps peppering across my skin. It was tantalizing.

"Purple is my favourite colour," he moaned as I rubbed my pelvis against his.

"Shut up, it is not."

The lopsided smile on his face was hard to read, and I had no idea if he was telling the truth or not, but I didn't care to find out. His magical hands had my bra unhooked in no time, and the cool air blowing across my chest, made my nipples stand at attention.

"Damn."

I arched my back and elongated my neck, and Zachary did not disappoint. He kissed down my collar bone and took his time making sure to not play favourites with either breast; it was enough to make me scream out in ecstasy. I bucked my hips and pushed against him, practically begging him to hurry up and get to the good stuff.

His warm hands were a wonderful contrast to the chilly breeze, as was his hot mouth. No doubt there were streaks of heat trailing down over my chest, across my shoulders, and under my chin, a spot he kissed that practically derailed me with the powerful sensations it sent out. That was new.

Not to be the only one topless, I pulled his shirt free of his body and gasped. His chest was beautiful, gorgeous, and firm, but there was a section just below his pecs where a white line stretched across and up, like a Mercedes emblem.

"That's my incision."

I ran my fingers over it, my gaze jumping back and forth from his eyes to the scar. "From what?"

"A liver transplant a few years ago."

The scar wasn't fresh, rather a faded pink line against an otherwise healthy skin tone.

"Oh? Are you okay?"

"Never better." He continued to look deep in my eyes, no sign of worry, not an ounce of trepidation.

"And you'll be fine?"

"Constantly beating the odds. I like it that way." He wiggled his eyebrows and then bucked his hips.

My eyes ran the length of the scar, and back up to his handsome face. "You're sure?"

"Yes. It was a touch of cancer, but they got it out. I get full body checkups all the time, and I'm fine. No reoccurrence. Healthy as a horse."

Staring into his deep gaze, I trusted in his words, not sure exactly what a *touch of cancer* meant, but if it was gone, then I had to believe him. "For sure?"

"Absolutely."

I swallowed, not really wanting to kill the mood, but curiosity was going to do me in if I didn't at least ask. "Your ex, is that why you broke up?"

"Definitely not. She had a midlife crisis, and decided I wasn't going to be part of the new life she wanted." The hint of a frown and the way his shoulders sagged had more tone and pitch than the words he just said, almost like it was an elevator pitch he'd practised so he could say it without feeling.

"And you're okay with that?"

He threaded his fingers through my hair and pulled me close. "Let me show you just how okay I really am."

I had my answers – for now, and with my head clear, my instincts took over. "Oh, please do."

He lifted and flipped me onto my back, slowly, seductively removing my boots, and moving his hands up my calves. When he reached my waistband, he inched my leggings down, but kept my underwear in place, even if *I* was suddenly ready to rip it free from my body.

"Ah, more purple. I love it. So beautiful."

The clouds to my left darkened more intensely, and a hint of rain reached the tip of my nose. It was coming.

"We should get inside." Of course, my mind hadn't fully shut off yet.

"Afraid of a little rain?"

"No, but what comes with it." So far though, no thunder.

"If you want." He was poised to move.

But I didn't really want to. "You know what, let's not let this moment pass."

He was so gentle, and yet so tenderly thorough in his exploration of my body, only tugging off my g-string with his teeth when I started to remove them myself. He pushed out of his chinos, putting his nakedness on full, fantastic display.

"Damn, yourself, Zachary. You are so fine." I purred with a sense of urgency on the tip of my tongue. "There's a condom in the pocket of my leggings."

It never hurt to come prepared.

He fiddled but quickly found the foil wrapper, tearing it open with his teeth before rolling it down his length.

I was panting as he teased me, inching between my legs on his knees as I arched up to welcome him in. Slowly, he caressed my inner thighs, making sure I was more than ready, and he moved in, connecting us. It was beyond pleasurable.

The breeze blew across my skin. Tiny drops of rain danced on my chest. Whispered words, and his thumbs touching me in the perfect spot, was enough to make me lock my ankles behind his back and dig my nails into his shoulders as I released moments before he did. His shudder rocked deep inside, and he collapsed upon me just as the clouds unleashed a steady downpour.

Chapter Six

I buried myself under Zachary, but it was no use. The rain came so fast and furious, everything was soaked in seconds.

We broke our carnal connection, and he backed up under the lip of the roof.

"Care to watch the storm roll in?"

"Not really."

"I promise I'll make it interesting, and safe." He opened his arms and his legs, allowing me to crawl in between, and grabbed the folded blanket he'd tossed out earlier.

"Usually, after," I let the word hang there, hoping he understood I meant after doing the deed, "I shower and get dressed before I cuddle."

Under the wrapped blanket, he kissed the side of my neck, and his strong thighs held me tight. "Well, if that's what you prefer…"

When he lifted the blanket an instant breeze of cool, rain-tinged air rushed under, almost chilling me to the bone.

"I'd prefer this. It's warmer." I pushed my back against his chest.

The rain continued to drench us, but somehow it was as highly charged as I was. I wrapped my ankles around his legs, opening up to the fresh air as a rumble of thunder rolled in the distance and thundered in my heart.

His hands roamed over my chest, holding me close. Slowly, as he continued to kiss my neck, his hand slipped under my arm, across my belly, and dropped between my legs.

"Oh, god," I called out as he touched me. His hands had cooled slightly in the rain.

His other hand joined in the fun, first rubbing my hip, and then the top of my thigh, before popping into the heat flowing out of me.

I arched my neck, feeling his kisses and nibbles while his fingers played and stroked and rubbed and caressed until my breath hitched deep in the back of my throat. He teased and groaned in my ear, making my core the center of his undivided attention. Good lord it was wonderful, and as the sensations built to higher and higher levels, I pushed my shoulders harder into his chest, the rain dancing across more and more of my skin. It was heavenly. And orgasmic. A violent shudder wracked my body just as a rumble sang out across the sky.

Breathless – my chest heaving uncontrollable – I melted into his arms.

"That was…"

"I know." I felt his smile against my cheek as a new warmth flowed and filled in the cracks of my heart.

We stayed that way until the storm passed us by, and the skies darkened further. For a moment, I thought we'd both fallen asleep as the embrace we were in was warm, safe, and relaxing.

However, with the approaching storm, huddled together buck naked wasn't my idea of a fun time. My clothes were drenched, as were his, but uncomfortably, we pulled them on.

"I'll take you to your hotel, you can grab a change of clothes, and then we'll head to my place for a shower before you take me out for that dinner you promised."

"I like the sound of that."

I awoke in the morning, snuggled into his chest, my fingers tracing the scar across his abdomen. Eventually, Zachary stirred.

"That tickles," he groaned, his voice raw and gravelly. He rolled over and kissed me. "Thanks for last night. *That* was the best night I've had in Cheshire Bay."

"Me too, although we never did make it out for dinner." My stomach growled at the thought of food, something hardy and full of protein.

The warm shower in my house had kept us from heading out to eat temporarily, and then we dried off on my couch, eventually moving into the bedroom to give my mattress a workout, until waves of sleepiness pulled us under.

"I'd love to take you out for breakfast but my flight back to the mainland comes in a couple of hours."

Right. He got nauseous on planes and needed the morning flight. "When will you be back?"

He rolled into a sitting position, not answering my question. "Where did I put my bag?"

"Living room, I think."

Giving me a full show, cute cheeks and all, he sauntered out of the bedroom, disappearing down the hall.

Grabbing my housecoat from the back of the door, I tossed it on, and followed, watching him jump into his pants, leaving them unfastened.

"You never answered my question."

"About?"

"Coming back?" A sudden sourness filled the pit of my stomach.

"Oh yeah, well, I'll let you know." He pulled on a sweater and walked closer to me. "What's with the face?"

"You're leaving."

"But I'll be back."

"But you don't know when? How is that? You just bought a house here, figured you'd be fast tracking things to get settled." I tried not to whine.

"There's a million things I need to cross off my ever-growing to-do list first." His hands wrapped around my shoulders. "But I am coming back. I promise. I have a few things I need to deal with."

"Like book your movers?"

"That's one thing, yes, but it's not just as simple as that. There are many legalities and things to sort out, and I have a few business meetings coming up as well." He slipped his watch on and tapped the face. "I'm sorry to just have to dash like this, but I need to get going. Can I call you later?"

"You'd better." Somehow, I didn't believe he would. "Oh, do you want me to drive you back to your motel?"

"It's not that far a walk, and besides, it's good for me to learn my way around this town, right?"

I nodded, my heart splintering with each ticking minute, and the abrupt change in his demeanour. Deep down I'd hoped we were building something special, but in this moment, I worried it was just an illusion.

"You okay?"

I put my best face on, the one I gave clients when the

countered deal wasn't the best, but it was the best they were going to get. "I'm good."

He brushed his lips over mine, slowly at first, but quickly building to a crescendo. A kiss like promised way more than he could offer at the moment. "Talk to you soon?"

"Yeah." I rolled my bottom lip between my teeth as he opened my front door and walked out.

No goodbyes from either of us. Maybe I was reading too much into it. But maybe not.

Closing the door, I leaned against it, looking up to the ceiling. What was wrong with me? Why was my heart aching? Why did him leaving wreck me so?

"Get a grip," I told myself as I wandered back to my bedroom and put on my running clothes.

Lacing up my Reebok, I headed out, almost hoping to find Zachary and beg him to stay, or maybe take me with him, however, my path this morning took me by Ashley's place, and like I'd wanted, she was returning home. I wanted to tell her about Zach and pick her brain.

"Hey, Ash." I called out and crossed the street in six easy jumps.

She was breathless and beet red, her workout over, and she greeted me accordingly. "Hey. Mia."

"What trail did you hit?"

"Lighthouse way."

"Nice. I'll check it out." I jumped from left to right foot, keeping my heart rate up. "By the way, I sold the Lowell place."

"That's great." She panted and placed her hands on her thighs. "To that mega builder?"

I gave her a quizzical look and stopped my mini jumps. "No, to that guy I was telling you about the other day."

"Oh. Isn't he the mega builder?" She wiped a bead of sweat from her forehead when she stood up.

"What mega builder?" I tipped my forehead closer to her and put my hands on my hips, my feet frozen to the ground.

"Just something I overheard late last night. About how someone was coming to town and had plans to build a resort. Even the mayor was talking about. She's quite excited."

"Who would that be? Who's this mega builder? And what resort? Cheshire Bay doesn't need a resort."

She looked everywhere but at me and kicked at the ground. "I don't remember the name. It was some corporation." She inhaled sharply. "Like NightingGale Holdings or something. It was a weird name, and I don't know if the resort is even in town. Could be on the beach, I missed that detail."

Relief washed over me. For a heartbeat I'd been terrified Zachary had had a hand in it. Then it hit me. The lack of wanting to explore the house, the bigger interest in the land. Suddenly, I saw the full name briefly on the bottom of one of the forms, and a lightbulb went off over my head, however it was glowing red. "Was it Newton-Garcia Holdings?"

She snapped her fingers. "Yes, that sounds right. Presented the mayor with a stack of papers."

"For the Lowell place?" My heart was beating in the back of my throat, and a fresh burst of adrenaline was responsible for the latest uptick in heartrate.

"I don't remember exactly, but we're meeting about it soon. Oh shit, I need to get going. I have an appointment in thirty minutes."

"Ashley Jones, you're not supposed to keep secrets from me." I yelled as she jogged away.

She waved but before she was out of sight, I did a

complete 180 and headed in the other direction, making good time to the mayor's office.

Taking the steps two at a time, I breathlessly ascended the stairs and rapped my knuckles with some controlled force on the door, before I pushed it open and stormed inside.

"Rachel, is Tonya in?" I skipped right over the pleasantries. With my compression leggings and an activewear shirt with a puffer vest, I wasn't exactly the image of a professional, however, the escalating pitch of my voice meant business.

"Yeah," she deadpanned. "She's here."

"Can I see her? Please?" I added as an afterthought.

"Mayor Vasquez is busy." She glared through her circular glasses.

"Can you check if she has a quick opening, please?"

She flipped aggressively through the calendar beside her keyboard. "She doesn't have an opening until next week."

"I think she'll see me." I should've stopped by Sylvia's Bakery and grabbed her a drink. Grabbed both Tonya *and* Rachel a drink.

"She's busy. You know how the mayor is."

"It'll be five minutes. I don't think five minutes is too much to ask, is it? Just one quick call." Did I dare pull the *but-I'm-a-tax-payer* card? I stared at the phone, willing her to challenge me.

Raising a brow into her dark hair sprinkled with greys and whites, she lifted the receiver and pressed a button. "Madam Mayor, Mia MacDonald is here to see you. I see. Thank you." A frown flipped her sardonic smile on its face, she rose and walked toward the door. "She's got two minutes for you." There was a lot of emphasis on the two.

"Thanks." Normally, I liked Rachel, but today she rubbed me the wrong way. Maybe she truly needed a coffee. With lots of maple sugar and whip cream.

I closed the door behind me, shutting a surprised Rachel away from the mayor and me. "Hey, Tonya."

"Mia. What do I owe you for this unexpected visit?" The mayor's dark eyes stayed focused on the papers scattered on her desk.

"I heard a rumour, and figured it was best to come here and get the truth."

"Oh." Her gaze connected with mine.

"Am I hearing correctly that a *mega builder*," to use Ashley's term, "was buying property in town?"

"You know, Miss MacDonald, that I can not discuss that with you." Using my last name was never a good sign. She rose and removed her glasses, walking around to the front of her desk. "But I can tell you, you are more than welcome to attend a town council meeting on the fifteenth. All matters involving the town will be openly discussed at that time."

"Is it the Lowell place?" And here I'd been going on and on to Zachary about how perfect our town was, and totally hyping it up, making it look even more attractive for someone who wanted to build a resort.

He'd played me, and the fool I was, I fell into his trap. Hook, line, and sinker.

My love for Cheshire Bay outshone my pride. "You can't honestly agree to this? Think of what it will do to our infrastructure? Knocking down the Lowell Place and building some sort of resort will wreck this town, not enhance it the way you think. Think of the increase of traffic and the noise; it'll drop the housing values of the strip to a fraction of what they are. It's a bad idea all around."

"There are many steps that would have to be taken first. It's not as easy as simply erecting a building. There are permits, and rezoning applications, and all of that takes time. Years sometimes."

"Think of the long range, Tonya. The big picture. It's a bad idea." My pleading voice arrived front and centre like a petulant child's.

Like a mother who'd had enough and wasn't giving an inch, she leaned against the edge of the desk and crossed her hands over her chest. "The fifteenth, Miss MacDonald. Can I expect to see you there?"

A stupid snort blew out of me. "Oh yes, and I'll be bringing reinforcements."

I knew some of the residents on the strip, like Eric and Jesse, plus I was going to tap into the STN and get the gossip. For sure, the old timers had their ears on everything, and likely overhead the conversation Mr. Newton-Garcia had in the pub.

Zachary may have toyed with my heart, but over my dead body will he toy with my town.

Chapter Seven

fter doing some digging, and it wasn't hard because despite Mayor Vasquez's insistence for me to show up at the meeting, a lot of information was public record. Plus, I had copies of the papers.

In my discovery, I learned Zachary Newton-Garcia was the CEO of a landowner investment company – a business that scouts out locations, buys the property and sells it to a developer. A few hours into my search, I'd also read he'd purchased many properties along various coastal cities and sold them to the highest bidder, but none on Vancouver Island. Yet.

Most of his sales went on to do well, and some flopped – like the one he sold in rural Oregon. The resort never went ahead as the townspeople protested the changes, and the mayor fought against the company, even though the land had been rezoned prior to the purchase. Of course, that didn't affect Zachary per-se, but it likely hampered that company from buying from him again. However, because the resort developers were mostly big names brands buying the property from Zachary, the large money carrot they dangled before the town councils was enough to entice most to accept the offer and to bump up whatever infrastructure was needed. And sadly, much to my detriment, it also boosted the local economy, as it changed the town.

Cheshire Bay was different. It was older, and based on the location of the Lowell property, building a resort would be very disruptive to the nearby residents, and the whole infrastructure of roadways, power and water and waste, not to mention all the damage to the local flora and fauna. There was no way Mayor Vasquez would accept the rezoning permit required. She couldn't. She loves the town almost as much as I do, although I was prepared to fight for it, especially if she wasn't.

Armed with the knowledge of what Zachary was planning, I arrived at the airport to confront him. And maybe give him a bit of a warning. Or... maybe I just missed him and couldn't wait to see him again. It was all so very confusing.

Through our clipped conversations, I'd never let on I knew his dastardly plans, and he never said anything about it, and it was so hard to not call him out on it too. When questioned once more about when he booked his movers, he was tight lipped, and to me, that confirmed it. He hadn't booked movers because *he* wasn't moving.

The day of the town council meeting, I stood impatiently in the waiting area of the Cheshire Bay airport. Zachary's flight was inbound, and my good friend Eric, who lived on the strip below the Lowell place, was the charter pilot. Not to be one to gossip without the full facts – even if I did enjoy listening to the Small Town Network – I told Eric, and his neighbour Jesse, it would be in their best interests to attend the town meeting, and for them to rally their neighbours too. When pressed, I became like the mayor, and didn't say anything to give it away. At least not much. Just a hint of things to come.

A crackle filled the small waiting area, announcing the arrival of the flight from Vancouver and I whipped my head to the windows to watch.

Cedar, the ticket agent, walked over. "They're almost here. Touchdown within a couple of minutes."

I stopped my pacing for a moment. "Thanks."

"Can I get you anything while you wait?"

"Nah, I'm good. Just anxious to see someone." I walked to the bank of windows and scanned the horizon, although I wasn't sure anxious was the right word. There were so many feelings and emotions swirling inside of me, I wasn't sure which would present itself first. "Which direction are they coming from?"

Not that it mattered. The runaway stretched out to the left and right of the windows, but because it was a small, charter-based airport, the plane usually parked in front of the waiting area and unloaded in plain sight.

"Let me check." She radioed over the walkie-talkie, and the response from the other side provided my answer.

They were coming in from the ocean side. Perfect. That gave Zachary a bird's eye view of the area and just added more desirable reasons to park a resort in my small town.

Nubs of anger flared deep inside, and my pacing turned into stomps as I pounded back and forth by the windows, glaring to the horizon with each pass.

I hated being used and hated how I had foolishly started feeling something for this guy. First second date in years, will never see a third.

Finally, the small plane came in for a landing and blew past the building.

"Flight CB6041 has arrived." Cedar hooked the walkie-talkie onto her belt and stopped beside me. "The plane will be here shortly and will park about there."

She pointed to the empty space in front of us.

I'd only flown out of Cheshire Bay once, and that was to catch a flight to Vancouver, and then an international flight out of there. Typically, since we only catered to charter flights, it was normally too expensive to fly across Vancouver Island. Driving across the island, paying ferry fees, and parking at the international airports was still cheaper overall. However, Zachary was loaded and mega-rich and could easily afford a chartered flight. Probably had his own personal jet too but didn't want to let that fact slip.

Cedar and her mechanic partner, Mitch, were long time friends of the pilot. Had Eric said anything to them about a rezoning application for a resort?

Should I encourage them to come by the town meeting this afternoon? "If you don't have plans at four, there's a meeting—"

"There they are." Cedar brushed her hands down the front of her dress and adjusted her hair clip. "Oh, I'm sorry, you were saying?"

"Talk to Eric. There's a town hall meeting today."

"Oh, those are so boring." She waved away the very idea and grabbed a basket of water bottles and fresh muffins with Sylvia's Bakery logo on them. "Excuse me."

While she propped open the door, readying for the passengers, I steeled myself, and inhaled sharply.

Two passengers only, and Zachary was one of them, walking the length of the small plane to the door, and down the fuselage steps onto the tarmac behind an older woman.

Damn, he gave a true runway model a run for his money – sexy as hell with a bit of scruff on his cheeks, and his suit looked tailored and expensive. Like more than my mortgage payment expensive.

He grabbed a suitcase, then another, and rolled toward the opened door where Cedar greeted him and welcomed him to Cheshire Bay. As he stepped into the waiting area, his focus connected with me, and his smile brightened the whole area.

Seeing it caused my breathing to increase with joy. A girl could get used to that if I wasn't feeling so betrayed.

"Mia." With long, easy strides, he hurried over to me and set his bags down, wrapping me in a hug before brushing his full lips over mine. "I've missed you."

"Hey," I said, pushing back a little, as my heart fluttered in response to the kiss. Damn, he was so handsome, and he smelled divine too.

He stared into my eyes. "When I told you what flight I was on, I didn't mean for you to pick me up. I can hail a cab. Did you miss me that much? I was only gone ten days."

Oh, the ego, even if there was truth in it. I did miss him, in a weird sort of way, but I didn't miss the sneaky things he was about to unleash on my town.

I couldn't hold back anymore. "Actually, I came here ready for a battle."

"Good god, why?" His face went blank.

"I know."

He tipped his head forward and his eyes widened, confusion tightening his brows together. "What do you know?"

I put my foot down and glared into his eyes, hoping my dulled daggers were stabbing his heart so he could feel what I felt when I uncovered the truth. "Were you ever planning on telling me?"

"Telling you what?"

I talked over him. "Or was I just the local tourist attraction? Someone stupid you managed to charm and weasel into your bed, or your deck as you would have it. Did you think I wouldn't find out?" My voice started to pitch. "About who you really are?"

He inhaled sharply and his Adam's apple bobbed. "Can we go somewhere private and talk?"

"You used me." I backed away and looked over his shoulder.

Cedar and Mitch huddled together, whispering, and staring in our direction. Eric soon joined them and took in the scene I was causing. Good. They needed to hear the truth.

Zachary glanced behind him and lowered his voice. "Can we please take this outside?"

"You lied to me, and then encouraged me to tell you all about the property and the town. *My* town. My *beloved* small town. You went behind my back and applied for rezoning permits. You had no intention of ever moving into the Lowell place. Why couldn't you tell me that?"

That perked Eric's ears and he stepped closer.

Zachary's expression fell onto the floor with a slump.

"You want to turn it into a resort. You want to ruin my small town. And I gave you the fucking keys to do it." My finger connected with his chest, and for a micro-second I worried I'd hit his scar, but that was a bit lower. Hopefully.

I stormed away and paused when my hand hit the handle of the door. My car was parked just outside, but I wasn't quite finished saying all that I needed to say.

Spinning around, I yelled. "You used me to further your business. You took my heart, the one I had just decided to give you, and you wrecked it with your deception. You messed with the wrong gal, and now you have a fight on your hands because I'm going to protest the ever-loving shit out of your applications and make sure this town knows what happens when a resort is built."

He went bug eyed but hadn't moved. It was like his feet were encased in cement.

"I read what happened to Clearwater Grove, and you're not selling the Lowell place to the highest bidder so they can destroy my town. You need to take your business elsewhere."

There, I said what I wanted to say, and seeing the sadness crinkle his eyes crushed my soul. Until I found out what business he was in, I had really enjoyed his company, and I loved so many parts about him, and I hated how I was hurting him. But he had hurt me too. All's fair in love and war, right?

I stomped out to my car and was just about in when Zachary burst through the door, the handle hitting the back of the wall with a solid whack.

"Mia, wait."

"Is it true?" The words were sharp on my tongue.

He stood there, shifting on his feet, but his gaze was firmly locked on me. "You need to know—"

"Is. It. True?" I had one foot in the car, ready to go.

His shoulders fell. "Yes."

I growled and jumped into my car, slamming my door so hard the window rattled in the frame. I tore out of the parking lot, pedal to the metal, and wearing the tread off my tires, but I was ready for a fight.

Town council was at four, and I was going to have front row seats.

Chapter Eight

With a thick stack of papers tucked into multiple folders, I occupied two chairs with my rebuttal, and sat sternly, crossing and re-crossing my legs as other town residents filtered into the school gym. Mayor Vasquez had moved the meeting to a larger location due to the rumblings going on, knowing full well the little conference room in her space wasn't going to work as it did normally.

As it was, ten minutes before the meeting started, all two hundred of the chairs were filled, and residents were starting to line against the back wall. The energy in the space was electric.

Yep, this was important. That made a little sunshine in my cloudy heart.

Two minutes before four, the two council members, including Ashley, walked to the makeshift table, and sat on the rigid plastic chairs, covering their whispers as they chattered.

At precisely four, Mayor Vasquez stood at the podium and tapped the mic, calling the room to order and for the guests to hush. An audible sigh echoed through the gymnasium.

She addressed the crowd, and read out the timetable for

this afternoon's meeting, letting us all know the elephant in the gym would be the last thing discussed.

I had at least thirty minutes to prepare, and spent those painstaking minutes reorganizing my papers, making sure certain documents were easy to grab.

Eventually, the regular administrative crap that no one really cared about was done, and the crowd slowly came to life.

Mayor Vasquez stood at the mic and looked to her council members. "We're all good?"

Ashley and Dominic nodded, and he passed something to Ashley, who connected with me.

"Okay then." Mayor Vasquez released a heavy sigh and shot a pointed look in my direction. "Let's address the rumours."

"May I?" A male voice piped up from behind everyone.

In the echoey space, a sniff was loud, so how he managed to sneak in with his high-end shoes and not alert anyone was a mystery. Not that I cared too much.

The crowd murmured as Zachary walked around them and stood at the podium. "Hello, everyone. I'm Zachary Newton-Garcia, and yes, I bought the Lowell place a couple of weeks back."

The volume of the crowd rose, and I sat smugly in my spot. Unfortunately, Zachary also had a self-satisfied smirk about him, and I wasn't super thrilled with that. He didn't seem the least bit bothered.

With ease and command, he continued. "Yes, I am the CEO of Newton-Garcia Holdings, and I work in conjunction with Resorts Plus, a major developer of resorts catering to hidden gems."

The noise escalated.

Zachary lifted his hand into the air and lowered it. "Please, let me speak and then I'll answer all and all questions."

Nasty names were tossed in his direction, but the crowd did eventually settle down.

"Not that anyone in this room should be surprised, but I did a random search of hidden gems, and this town surfaced, as did Stewart Surf."

A few boos rippled between people. There was a little friendly competition between the two towns in our minor league sports, and even though Stewart Surf was more of a touristy town, the Cheshire Bay residents never enjoyed sharing the same breath as Stewart Surf in any news, briefings, or discussions.

"We looked into that other town," Zachary connected with me, and I raised an eyebrow. One point to him for being able to read the crowd. "They didn't have what we were looking for, and that's when I discovered the listing for the Lowell place a couple of months ago."

I shifted in my seat and looked over at my friend Ashley, who was busy studying something in front of her.

Zachary wrapped his hands around the sides of the podium. "I talked back and forth with my real estate agent and sent a team of engineers to do a land study and provide me detailed inspection reports. The land itself was perfect for what my clients were looking for – ocean front property, small town charm, the works. It checked off many of the boxes."

I opened the folder and scanned over the first document, it wasn't needed, so I tucked it under the bottom of the stack.

"I flew in, did the final walk through, and officially became the owner, ready to transfer the title to Resorts Plus."

"You sold it already?" A gruff voice commanded.

"You didn't let me finish."

"So quit your dawdling and get to the meat of this."

A round of applause to the old guy, but really, if he had stopped interrupting, Zachary could've been finished by now.

"After meeting with the realtor, and being given a tour of the town, yes, I did submit an application to the mayor for rezoning purposes the day I took official possession." He shifted on his feet and scanned the crowd. He was unwavering, and not a lick of a worry christened his handsome face. "That's part of my process – I get the ball rolling and they take over. That being said, the process is always a long, tedious wait. However, I hadn't disclosed any of this to the developers as I was waiting until my meeting with them in person the next afternoon, but yes, I had started to put the ball in motion."

Another nasty name breezed out of someone, this time the owner was female.

"Then I spent a couple of nights here the charming little town as well as enjoying the property. It's lovely, and already I have wonderful memories of it." He threw a glance in my direction and my cheeks heated recalling that afternoon.

It was a fond memory for me too.

"Before I left, since I was staying at the Bay Western, I approached the owners, Mr. and Mrs. Bedfordshire, and I made an offer of development there instead."

"What? That's not much better." Another voice from deep in the crowd.

"But it is."

I had to agree with Zachary, as far as electricity, water, and waste management went, it was the better of the two options. They already had everything in place. But I hadn't heard any news of them having had an offer; I didn't even know the place was up for sale.

"They have the infrastructure to make it work. And we

wouldn't be making it a resort. I have the right connections to update it with new owners, and yet, still have it keep the Cheshire Bay charm."

"So, the resort people would still be moving in and changing our town?"

Zachary shook his head after raking his hands through it. "No. I have another investment company that's interested in redeveloping the motel, contingent on the Bedfordshire's accepting the offer."

I glanced around the gym. Were the Bedfordshires here? I hadn't noticed them, but then again, I wasn't looking for them either.

Mayor Vasquez stood beside Zachary. "Nothing changes, people. All that would happen is the motel would have new management, if the new buyer agrees to the all the terms and conditions. It would infuse a little freshness into the area and make it more hospitable for our treasured visitors. Mr. Newton-Garcia has in fact pulled the rezoning request for the Lowell place."

I stared open-mouthed at him, and after blinking a few times, I mouthed, "For real?"

He nodded.

"Is everyone clear on that? The Lowell place is now Mr. Newton-Garcia's, and the Bay Western motel is considering an offer from a different developer, is that correct?" She faced Zachary.

"That is correct."

"There's nothing to worry about. No major changes are coming to this town, so you can all rest easy. Cheshire Bay will not be invaded with resorts."

A collective sigh rumbled.

"Any other further concerns I need to address, or are we

good until the next meeting?" She scanned the gym, but no one spoke up. "Then we're done." She extended her hand to Zachary. "Welcome to Cheshire Bay."

They shook hands, and she joined Ashley and Dominic, shooting a brief smile in my direction.

I rose from my seat, tucking my papers into my bag. I didn't get the fight I wanted, but at least I'd been prepared. Running a quick look over the crowd, I spotted Eric. He gave me a thumbs up and a friendly nod before exiting the gym. Thank goodness he wasn't upset with me, although everything I had said was true. It was a sweet relief to not have to worry about the rezoning after all. I turned my attention back to the man of the moment.

Zachary chatted quickly with the council members, shaking their hands as well, before he sauntered over in my direction.

Hesitantly, he stopped a few feet short. "You didn't give me a chance to explain. At the airport."

Suddenly, I felt foolish and hung my head. My loose waves provided a bit of a curtain. "I'm sorry."

Stepping closer, he tipped up my chin with the pad of his finger and looked into my eyes. "I love your passion though; it was one of the first things I adored about you."

"Yeah. I can get a little over excited."

"Don't ever change that."

I swallowed and nodded. "Okay."

"Promise?"

"I promise." My gaze danced between his two eyes. "You're telling the truth? You're not selling the Lowell place to the highest bidder?"

"Nope." He popped the p sound. "After that magical

evening, I became a little selfish and didn't want anyone else to enjoy that view, that rain, that deck. I want that to be my place to entertain, to live in, to have special guests stay over."

My heart stopped, and I gave it a gentle smack to restart. I wanted those things too. "It is an amazing property. What happens to it now?"

"I was always the owner, which was never up for discussion, but I've also not put it on the table to the developers. It's mine. Clear title."

"Wow, how nice to not have a mortgage." Someday, that was my goal.

"Not complaining."

"And your place back in Vancouver? What about your job?"

He chuckled. "The job I can do anywhere. I travel a lot, scoping places out, so my home base can be wherever I want it to be."

"Anywhere? Like Cheshire Bay?" I cocked my eyebrow, waiting for his answer, the one I hoped he'd answer with a resounding and energetic yes.

"I'd actually prefer it." His warm gaze latched onto mine. "After I finish for the day, I can grab a beer and sit on my deck, enjoy that breathtaking view. My girlfriend could join me, and help me create new memories there, or in the house, or over dinner."

"Your girlfriend?" I narrowed my eyes until his smile threatened to burst across his face. "Oh, you mean…" I held my breath and released it, whispering a solitary, "Me?"

"If you'd be interested in the job."

I swatted his arm. "If you refer to it as a job, I'm one hundred percent out."

"Fine it's not a job, but the title is open, if you want try it out."

My heart sped wobbled. "Yes, I do. I really, really do."

"And I seriously think you should consider becoming mayor of this town when her term is up. Your passion is contagious, look at all the people you corralled into showing up. That's why I couldn't do it. I couldn't change the landscape of this place. It backfired in Clearwater Cover, badly, and that town never recovered. After watching you with this town, with these people, building a resort would do more damage than any financial benefits it could ever provide. I'll scope out Stewart Surf for resorts, or even Half Moon Bay. Do the whole if *you build it, they will come* thing, but not here."

"Half Moon Bay doesn't have much."

"So, things could only get better from there, right?" He tipped his forehead against mine. "Are we okay? Can I kiss you yet?"

"You'd better." I wrapped my arms around his neck and parted my lips a fraction as I breathed him in.

Never in my life had I had someone clap after I kissed someone, but in that gym, that afternoon, people clapped. All of them. It was the most endearing, heartfelt moment of my life… so far.

Epilogue

Five years later…

The cap to the first of numerous pill bottles twisted off easily, but the subsequent ones gave me a little trouble. They always had. In the end, I managed and put one of each pill into the glass dish and set it on the tray.

My true love was already out on the deck, overlooking the ocean as the sun as it began its nightly journey. It was our favourite place to watch the day come to an end, and in truth, making memories on the deck was a pleasurable activity, although limited lately.

Managing the tray, I ambled out to bring him his food and medication. Setting it down on the table beside him, I leaned down and gave him a kiss. It was never a quick brush of lips against lips, like a habit, and each time it had the power to make the butterflies soar.

I pulled back, stared into his gorgeous eyes, and ran my hand over his face. "You're still the one."

The lines had deepened over the past few months due to his health struggles and his eyes had sunken a bit from the weight loss, but he was still charming and handsome, and he held my heart in his hands.

Eleven years ago, he'd had a transplant due to liver cancer, and the transplant extended his life, but sadly, the nasty disease had returned. With a vengeance.

"Are you warm enough?" I asked.

He was huddled under a blanket and the overhead heater was on low, giving him his own pocket of warmth. "Shh. You'll wake her." Avoiding my question, he placed a kiss atop her head. "She's fine."

"And you?"

Naturally our four-month-old daughter, Sadie, was perfectly warm, chest to chest, she was snuggled against her daddy, her ear just above the rhythmic beating of his heart, but it was Zachary I was most concerned with. Hand on my hip, and a don't mess with me expression I had perfected over the years, I went to open my mouth.

"I'm good," he whispered before I could speak. "Please, sit."

"Time to eat." I curled beside him and pointed to the sandwich he could easily pick up with one hand and not disturb Sadie.

Begrudgingly, he reached for the thick lettuce-tomato-turkey sandwich and took a hearty bite. "Happy?"

"Always." I took in his face, trying to memorise every single line, every whisker, every fleck in the irises of his dual-coloured eyes, a trait our daughter did not inherit. At least not yet.

Sadie needed to know all the details about her father, because some day soon, well... it just wasn't talked about, but we both knew *someday* was coming.

A master of pill taking, he barely wet his palate with the water, and pop-pop-pop, the pills all went down.

I leaned against the backrest and admired the most amazing man I'd ever loved as he draped his arm around me.

Zachary had grown his company and, at my behest, avoided touching Cheshire Bay. The proposal for the Bay Western had been a vicious fight, and in the end, he'd let it go as they couldn't reach an agreement. After that, he'd kept his business dealings out of the area, even skirting around Stewart Surf, but did scoop up some land in Half Moon Bay. That area was sold to a hotel chain and was still in the design process last I checked.

As his health took a decline, I knew he wanted a child to love and hold, so I went off the pill, and lo and behold, a month later, the stick showed two lines. He was over the moon, and once I had accepted the news, so was I. I didn't think it would happen so quickly, but not a day has passed where I don't fall in love with her a little more. I didn't even know it was possible to do that with a child, although it happened with her father, my one true love. Amazingly enough, every day was better than the one before.

Our daughter was born a month early and christened Sadie Newton-Garcia, as when we eventually decided to legally tie the knot, I was taking Zachary's name without hesitation.

I snuggled against my family, and we faced the ocean.

The sun was inching lower and painting the overhead skies with the most magnificent soft hues of pinks, purples, and blues. In half an hour, the ball of light would touch the horizon.

"She's going to love sunsets, right?" He cleared his throat.

Sadie wiggled from the movement but didn't wake.

"She absolutely will. What's not to love?" I reached for his hand, and pressed a kiss into the palm, rolling it closed, and holding it tight.

"I've thought about our wedding," he said, shifting a little, "and I want it here. On the deck. At sunset."

"It's a big deck, but I don't think it'll fit all our friends and family."

"No, it won't, but maybe it should be a smaller event, like just between us and a couple of witnesses, and a justice of the peace. We've been putting it off for far too long." There was a seriousness in his eyes, and I was slightly concerned for the sudden rush to sign matrimonial papers.

"No family?" I swallowed.

Mine would be pissed to miss it, his too. The Normandys had practically adopted Zachary into the mix, loving him like a son and not an outsider, and my siblings loved and adored him. My parents wanted the whole wedding package, with Dad walking me down the aisle. Both were surprisingly a little ticked when we had Sadie before any talk of wedding vows.

"We can do a big deal later, but right now, I just want to be married to you in the eyes of the law, and we can do the grand celebration later... Before..." He looked off into the distance.

Yeah, I didn't want to say it either.

I nodded emphatically. "Yes. Let's do it. How about tomorrow? I can make a few calls, talk to the mayor."

"No need." He reached for his phone, opened his messages, and hit send. "Will five minutes work?"

"What?" My jaw unhinged. "But I'm not dressed. You're not... Sadie..."

"You have that beautiful dress in the closet, but I honestly don't care what you wear. You're beautiful the way you are right now, in my plaid shirt and the leggings with spit up on them. It's perfection." He waved a finger between us. "This is us. Laid back, relaxed, a little bit of heaven on earth. Why should we dress it up and change it?"

He had a point, although it was small. All my life I had

dreamed of a big production wedding, with the princess dress. Mind you, I'd also dreamed of having a husband until we were ninety. Some things change.

"We can do big for the reception down the line, but for this, I just want the formal part to be us." He opened his arm up, and I snuggled in, breathing in his everything to the tiniest molecule in my soul.

"Okay," I whispered breathlessly, fighting back a sudden rush of tears. "I'm totally on board with this. I want to be your wife." Even if by all intents and purposes, in the eyes of the law we already were, but I understood the formality of signing the declaration. "I love you, Zachary."

He kissed my forehead. "I love you more, Mia. I can't imagine my world without you in it."

"Me either." The tears swelled and burst free of their hold.

He squeezed me and rested his head against mine. "You're not supposed to cry on your wedding day."

"They're tears of joy," I promised.

A commotion of noise came from the bottom of the deck.

"Up here," Zachary whispered as loudly as he could.

"They're here? Already?" I wiped my eyes as Eric and Lily, our neighbours who lived on the strip below us, crested the top of the stairs with Mayor Vasquez.

After a few quick waves and greetings, I helped Zachary onto his feet, and wrapped my arm through his. If he wanted a ceremony at sunset, we'd best start now. Time was running out. Quickly.

The sun was setting, the bottom just caressing the horizon, and the final rays of sunlight stretched out in golden tones and shades of warm amber. Glittery waves moved along, darkening as they approached the beach.

It was perfection, until I looked into Zachary's eyes. There was my heaven. He was my hope, my dreams, my future, and I promised to love him forever.

I squeezed his arm. "God, I love you Zachary."

"I love you, Mia. You make me a better man." He cradled Sadie close, who stretched and moaned. "And I love you too, my little miss Sadie."

Tears streamed down my cheeks as Mayor Vasquez began.

"Dearly beloved, we are gathered here today…"

~~~~

The Cheshire Bay Series

RETURN to CHESHIRE BAY

It's hard to start over, and find love, when no one forgets your past.

Pregnant and suddenly jobless, Lily is desperate to figure out what she wants from life before the baby comes. Leaving her busy, high-rise life on hiatus, she sets out to the small-town on the Pacific coast determined to fix up the family's summer home and sell it for some much-needed cash flow.

As she begins the renovations, she becomes reacquainted with her sexy neighbour, a charter pilot, who now lives on the strip all year long. Despite his charm and laid-back attitude, Eric's a distraction she doesn't need right now. Besides, there's no way he could possibly be attracted to the single mom-to-be, right?

Despite her repeated attempts to show she's changed, Cheshire Bay refuses to welcome her home. Will she cave to the mounting pressure to return to the high-rise lifestyle, or will she put the rumours to rest and make Cheshire Bay – and Eric – her new home?

ADRIFT in CHESHIRE BAY

She's ready to surprise her boyfriend. Turns out she's going to be the one in shock.

Tonight's the night. Cedar couldn't be more excited to announce to her long-time sweetheart, at their anniversary dinner, that she's expecting. That is until a mysterious woman shows up at their work, looking for Mitch, to introduce him to a young boy, their son.

With her plans up in smoke, Cedar doesn't know what to do next. When Mitch shuts down and refuses to discuss his past, she risks everything to uncover details that had changed her future. In the middle of it all, her soulmate discloses how he never wanted kids. Heartbroken, Cedar is forced to plan a new future.

But Mitch means the world to her. Can she forgive and forget? Will she move on without him? Or will she always be adrift in a sea of what could've been?

AWAKE in CHESHIRE BAY

An emergency landing, a sexy stranger, and a night she's never going to forget.

Amber has never been lucky in love, that's why her guard is way up. Her bar and her small-town life are all she needs. That is until a plane has to make an emergency landing at the local airport, and a handsome stranger blows into her quiet life.

She pours the mysterious Mr. Welsh a drink, and he wins her over with his charm, and sexy accent. He extends a request for her hand at dinner, and she accepts. What was only supposed to be a warm Cheshire Bay welcome for the unexpected guest turns out to be a star-filled night full of sizzling chemistry neither of them wants to end.

As the sun crests the horizon, reality dawns. Now that she's had a taste of what a true gentleman is like, she's terrified of what happens when the sun rises and it's time for him to leave.

CHRISTMAS in CHESHIRE BAY

Can a Christmas miracle happen even if you don't believe in the magic?

Mona has never gotten over her last visit to the family's summer beach home thirteen years ago. That was the heartbreaking day her beloved mother passed away. Now, with her sister planning a beach wedding on Christmas Day, Mona must confront her past. All of it. No matter how much it hurts.

Upon arrival to her family's summer home, a twist of fate has her in desperate need of a plan B. In walks Jesse, the sweet-- and handsome--next door neighbor, offering up a guest room in his house. Jesse's the type of guy that believes in the magic of Christmas, and wants to remind Mona what it's all about, even if she's not so sure she has any belief left.

But like Mona, Jesse hides beneath his own scars and secrets. Can these two help each other heal old wounds even when their past hurts resurface? Will Mona be able to drop her walls and embrace the magic of the season and finally heal the damage from Christmas' past?

JOURNEY to CHESHIRE BAY

A homeless dropout with nothing to live for. A socially inept astrophysicist with a detailed future. A cross-country journey that will forever alter their lives.

Iris is ready to clean up her life and start over. For real this time. No more drinking, homelessness, or failed suicide attempts. Her only viable solution is to ditch her past and move across the country to the small town of Cheshire Bay. As she boards her only means of escape, she's gobsmacked to see her seatmate is the nerd she tormented back in high school.

Holden has put the past behind him, including those awful years in high school where he was picked on for being smarter and younger than his peers. Grown up and filled out, he's ready to live his meticulously planned future, forty-four hours from takeoff. However, he has to get there first. That, unfortunately, includes a six-hour flight beside the girl who made his high school life a nightmare.

When the plane makes an emergency landing and the clock starts ticking, book smart Holden needs street smart Iris's help to get him home. Maybe together they can put their differences aside and navigate the challenges ahead. Maybe, just maybe, the road trip will change their view on the other forever.

94

CHARMED in CHESHIRE BAY

No kissing, no dating, and no matter what, absolutely no falling in love.

These are three rules Summer Bates has vowed to honour after losing her one true love. Used as a pawn since then, both romantically and professionally, she's sworn off all men and moved to the small town of Cheshire Bay to start over. In life. In business. But definitely not in love.

Until she has a one-night stand with the gorgeous bookstore owner.

Adam Normandy is the epitome of a small-town homespun hero, all wrapped in a sexy package. Annoyingly charismatic, he pushes Summer's buttons. Including the one no one's touched in years. As much as she tries to resist, he's rousing new emotions she thought she'd never feel again. And she likes it.

However, Summer's past arrives with a vengeance, threatening to destroy her new career, her new life, and the budding romance with Adam. Can he be the hero she needs, or will she lose everything, including her happily ever after?

SECOND CHANCES in CHESHIRE BAY

Thirteen years apart. Two shattered hearts beyond repair. One shot at a second chance neither of them saw coming.

In a small town, the list of good-looking, age-appropriate, and *single* guys is already slim. Being the only doctor for miles, those choices become even narrower. When a speed dating event surfaces, Dr. Chloe Tarkin jumps at the chance to meet several eligible bachelors but is caught completely off guard when one in particular graces her table.

The guy who once held the key to her heart.

The other half of a pair of dreamers with big plans for their future.

The swoony gentleman her soul never forgot. Or forgave.

BJ Sutcliff moved to the bay area years ago to escape his past, his controlling family, and to focus on being who *he* wants to be. Never expected he'd run into anyone familiar. And he never imagined he'd run into the woman whose heart he shattered when he slammed the door on them all those years ago.

He's ready to make amends for the way he screwed up. This time, he's not settling for second best, but he'd jump at a second chance - if she can find it in her heart to let bygones be bygones. Or are some mistakes just too much to forgive and forget?

UNFORGIVEN in CHESHIRE BAY

Revenge is never a fool-proof plan.

Erin Normandy has learned to guard her heart and keep her secrets safely stashed away. When she's asked to design a huge mural and collaborate on the project with a handsomely rugged man, she jumps at the chance to say yes and impress. What a gift to her business, and her mounting debt. How could she refuse?

Until… she learns who he is.

Blissfully single, David Dean is surprisingly smitten by Erin's fierce tongue, her blunt honesty, and a willingness to call him on his bullshit, something no one has challenged before. It's intoxicating, and because she's a single mom, he wants to do right by her and treat her well, even if it comes across as old-fashioned.

Until… he learns who she is.

As his past business mistake collides with her aggressive social media smear, he starts to question their building attraction. Was any of it real?

While revenge may have been part of her plan, destroying a heart – especially the one she's fallen in love with – never was. Can they forgive each other or is the damage unrepairable?

FLIRTY in CHESHIRE BAY

An estranged sister, a flirtatious connection, and the one thing she never thought she'd lose – her heart.

Libby learns her donated kidney is no longer prolonging her estranged father's life. He needs another, and preferably from the sister she doesn't remember. Shocked, she's now tasked with reaching out and convincing this familial stranger to donate an organ. But how? She can't blurt it out. She needs to soften the blow. She needs a way in.

Enter the fun and devilishly flirty older man, Landon Morris.

As he sets his wise, ocean-blue gaze upon her, Libby fights against his charms, until she discovers his connection to her newfound sister. Suddenly, Landon has a lot more appeal, and she mirrors his flirtatious behaviour, until he's wrapped around her unintended finger, introducing her to his family and friends – and the older sister she never really had.

In the midst of her deceit however, Libby finds she's falling hard for Landon, and she worries the truth behind her actions will sabotage any future with him. Will her true feelings and intentions be enough to keep them together, or will she lose everything because she flirted with deception?

Checklist of reads

	Read	Own	Need
Run Away Charlotte	○	○	○
Ask Me Again	○	○	○
Duly Noted	○	○	○
That Summer	○	○	○
If You Say Yes	○	○	○
Serving Up Innocence	○	○	○
Serving Up Devotion	○	○	○
Serving Up Secrecy	○	○	○
Serving Up Hope	○	○	○
It All Began with a Note	○	○	○
It All Began with a Mai Tai	○	○	○
It All Began with a Wedding	○	○	○
Noel	○	○	○
Whistler's Night	○	○	○
Behind the Mask (eBook only)	○	○	○
Unmasking River (eBook only)	○	○	○
Return to Cheshire Bay	○	○	○
Adrift in Cheshire Bay	○	○	○
Awake in Cheshire Bay	○	○	○
Christmas in Cheshire Bay	○	○	○
Swept by Desire (eBook only)	○	○	○
Journey to Cheshire Bay	○	○	○
Charmed in Cheshire Bay	○	○	○
Second Chances in Cheshire Bay	○	○	○
Unforgiven in Cheshire Bay	○	○	○
Flirty in Cheshire Bay	○	○	○

Up to date listings on www.hmshander.com

about the author

USA TODAY bestselling author H.M. Shander is a stargazing, romantic at heart who once attended Space Camp and wanted to pilot the space shuttle, not just any STS – specifically Columbia. However, the only shuttle she operates in her real world is the #momtaxi; a reliable electric car that transports her two kids to school and various sporting events. When she's not commandeering Elektra, you can find the school librarian surrounded by classes of children as she reads the best storybooks in multiple voices. After she's tucked her endearing kids into bed and kissed her trophy husband goodnight, she moonlights as a contemporary romance novelist; the writer of sassy heroines and sweet, swoon-worthy heroes who find love in the darkest of places.

For all the latest release news, subscribe to H.M. Shander's newsletter through the website (www.hmshander.com), or you can follow her on Twitter(@HM_Shander), Facebook (hmshander).

Thank you for following her on this incredible journey.

www.ingramcontent.com/pod-product-compliance
Lightning Source LLC
Chambersburg PA
CBHW022043170626
46808CB00003B/1344